PRAISE FOR

M000187928

"Provocative entertainment."
—*Booklist*

"A bludgeoning celluloid rush of language and ideas served from an action-painter's bucket of fluorescent spatter."
—Alan Moore

"Wilson invokes not a dialogue with the reader but a bare-knuckle fistfight. Dizzying, disorienting, smooth and shocking. A rough, crunchy high."
—*Publishers Weekly*

"A new comprehensive standard. Wilson's insights reach to the furthest ends."
—Jonathan Lethem

"Pomo cybertheory never tasted so good!"
—*American Book Review*

"D. Harlan Wilson has found a new language festering on the dark side of the moon."
—Mark Amerika

"New bursts of stream-of-cyberconsciousness prose."
—*Library Journal*

"Wilson writes with the crazed precision of a futuristic war machine gone rogue."
—Lavie Tidhar

"Wonderfully demented. A thesaural explosion.
Gonzo prose for the information age."
—*Starburst Magazine*

"Fast, smart, funny."
—Kim Stanley Robinson

"An orgy of violence and absurdity written with surgical precision."
—*Entropy Magazine*

"Utterly original."
—Barry N. Malzberg

"If reality is a crutch, Wilson has thrown it away."
—*Rain Taxi*

"A brilliant data screen of future memories."
—Arthur Kroker

"Wilson is both a ghost in the machine and a spanner in the works."
—*The Rumpus*

"Kafka/Cronenberg on laughing gas.
Philip K. Dick/William Gibson on acid."
—Larry McCaffery

"D. Harlan Wilson is one of those rare voices in contemporary
fiction that deserves to be called incomparable."
—*Vol. 1 Brooklyn*

SCHREBER THEE₂ PSYCHOTIC DR

THE PSYCHOTIC DR. SCHREBER
Copyright © 2019 by D. Harlan Wilson
ISBN: 978-0-9991152-5-1
Library of Congress Data available on request

First paperback edition published by Stalking Horse Press, September 2019

All rights reserved. Except for brief passages quoted for review or academic purposes, no part of this book may be reproduced, stored in a retrieval system, or transmitted by any means without the written permission of the author and publisher. Published in the United States by Stalking Horse Press.

The characters and events in this book are fictitious or used fictitiously. Any similarity to real persons, living or dead, is coincidental and not intended by the author.

www.stalkinghorsepress.com

Design by James Reich

STALKING HORSE PRESS
Santa Fe, New Mexico

SCHREBER THEE PSYCHOTIC DR.

-D. HARLAN WILSON

STALKING HORSE PRESS
SANTA FE, NEW MEXICO

OTHER BOOKS BY D. HARLAN WILSON

NOVELS
Primordial: An Abstraction
Peckinpah: An Ultraviolent Romance
Blankety Blank: A Memoir of Vulgaria

THE BIOGRAPHIZER TRILOGY
Hitler: The Terminal Biography
Freud: The Penultimate Biography
Douglass: The Lost Autobiography

THE SCIKUNGFI TRILOGY
The Kyoto Man
Codename Prague
Dr. Identity, or, Farewell to Plaquedemia

FICTION COLLECTIONS
Natural Complexions
Battles without Honor or Humanity
Battle without Honor or Humanity: Volume 2
Battle without Honor or Humanity: Volume 1
Diegeses
They Had Goat Heads

DRAMA
Three Plays

NONFICTION/CRITICISM
J.G. Ballard (Modern Masters of Science Fiction)
They Live (Cultographies)
Technologized Desire: Selfhood & the Body in Postcapitalist Science Fiction

QUOTE

"In these landscapes lay a key."
—J.G. Ballard, *The Atrocity Exhibition*

DEDICATION

For the agents of pathology.

PRESCRIPTION

An oneiric stab.

DIALECTIC

Dementia Praecox. Precocious madness. Schizophrenia.

Nervensprache. Nerve-language.

Never-language.

SCHIZE

Varicose skyscapes. Superzero literature. *Choisisme.* Unwriting.
Unworlding.

THE PSYCHOTIC DR. SCHREBER

The title of Freud's 1911 seminal case study informs, if not coerces, the métier of this fleeting improvisation.

There is only one way to unpack it.

Sadly, the flowers have deliquesced in the humidity. Every word is a smudge of pollen.

Which brings us, at last, to the present zeitgeist.

FORWARDS

Dr. Flechsig stands at the top of the stairway like a broken reverie. In an alternate universe, the hot bitumen of his soul pours down the steps and tars the escarpment in an endless timelapse.

The patient crawls upwards with slow resolve. Each new wave of distillate suffocates him, tears the flesh from his neck and back. Sometimes he balks. Hands twisted into claws, he cranks his head and puts his ear to the marble, listening to the hum of the earth's core, glaring at the doctor in stylized hate.

"*Vorwärts.*"

It takes the patient over twenty minutes to reach the top. Dr. Flechsig records the event in an eelskin notebook, glyphing his syntax in a stenographic shorthand. Then he ushers the patient into the Devil's Castle . . .

A MONSTER IN THE WORLD'S HISTORY

From the Mountaintop: "I am the anti-ass *par excellence,* and on this account alone a monster in the world's history. For I come from heights into which no bird has ever soared; I know abysses into which no foot has ever slipped. A word from me is enough to drive all the evil instincts into a face" (858-59).
—Zarathustra, *Ecce Homo: How One Becomes What One Is*

THE RAIN AND THE SUNSHINE FROM ABOVE

From the Sewer: "They cannot represent themselves; they must be represented. Their representative must at the same time appear as their master, as an authority over them, as an unlimited governmental power that protects them against the other classes and sends them the rain and the sunshine from above" (608).
—Karl Marx, *The Eighteenth Brumaire of Louis Bonaparte*

HOMOSEXUAL LIBIDO

From the Underworld: "Homosexual libido." —Sigmund Freud, Multiple Case Studies

ORAL, ANAL, GENITAL

From the New Underworld: "It is obvious that the libido, with its paradoxical, archaic, so-called pregenital characteristics, with its eternal polymorphism, with its world of images that are linked to the different sets of drives associated with the different stages from the oral to the anal and the genital—all of which no doubt constitutes the originality of Freud's contribution—that the whole microcosm has absolutely nothing to do with the macrocosm; only in fantasy does it engender world" (92). —Jacques Lacan, *The Ethics of Psychoanalysis*

ÜBERSETZUNG, TRADUCTION, TRANSLATION

Nietzsche and Marx predated Daniel Paul Schreber insofar as their major works had been published before Schreber's first "nervous illness" (1884-85). Their assertions are largely decorative, although the scholarly figures cited in previous chapters are linked by Paul Ricoeur's "hermeneutic of suspicion," a concept presupposing that everything (a piece of writing, a mathematical equation, a slice of cake, an apocalypse, a covert glance, no glance at all, etc.) is a text subject to critical inquiry by an analyst who, as Ricoeur states in *Freud and Philosophy*, possesses a double motivation: "willing to suspect, willingness to listen; vow of rigor, vow of obedience" (27).

The present hermeneutic is no exception.

Freud never met Schreber; he read his memoirs and diagnosed his effigy. Born in 1901 at the apex of Schreber's second, longest, definitive breakdown (1893-1902), Jacques Lacan developed conclusions about Schreber based on his notorious "return to Freud." This retroaction certified his post-Freudian status, which hinged on the repossession and reproduction of Freud's original texts (especially his concept of ego psychology) through the filter of (post)structuralist modalities and, above all, language, *langue, sprache.*

Schreber perished during his third and final exodus from reality (1907-11). Lacan was 10 years old at the time of his death.

Between the ages of 54 and 55, Lacan hosted a seminar called *The Psychoses* in which he used Freud's model of Schreber as an index for his own approach to the psychotic apparatus, investigating Schreber's written account of his condition, *Memoirs of My Nervous Illness,* in tandem with Freud's case history, "Psychoanalytic Notes Upon an Autobiographical Account of a Case of Paranoia," better known in popular culture as "The Psychotic Dr. Schreber."

THE MAN WHO MELTED

An attendant of the country court melted into the mattress, "becoming one with his bed" (Schreber 103).

Daniel witnessed it from a cot on the far side of the room. He had been strapped down by a team of fleeting-improvised men, souls "transitorily put into human shape by divine miracles" (61).

More terrifying than being confined—or, for that matter, than witnessing the deliquescence—was the fact that the attendant, who enjoyed dressing in Daniel's clothes (103), had put on one of his suits before laying down to sleep.

The suit didn't melt; slowly it sunk into the sheets as the man seeped through the interstices of the fabric.

This happened on thousands of occasions. Nothing ever happened to Daniel once. Tormented by repetition, he longed for the Singularity.

It became apparent that the attendant was himself a fleeting-improvised man.

Everybody was a fleeting-improvised man, cast in the drama of his life by a devious collaborative of fathers, directors, clinicians, engineers, experimentalists, monsters and gods that, somehow, he would have to destabilize, override, dominate and kill.

This state of ubiquity did not include Daniel himself, as he deduces in the Book of Life.

"I can put this point briefly," he epiphanizes, "*everything that happens is in reference to me*" (233).

Here, then, is the axial Way Out.

THE PATHOLOGICAL HYMN OF SUBJECTIVITY

From the Book of Life: "I wish to add another point in connection with God's inability to understand the living human being as an organism and to judge his thinking correctly, which has in many ways become important to me. I can put this point briefly: *everything that happens is in reference to me.* Writing this sentence, I am fully aware that other people may be tempted to think that I am pathologically conceited; I know very well that this very tendency to relate everything to oneself, to bring everything that happens into connection with one's own person, is a common phenomenon among mental patients. But in my case the reverse obtains. Since God entered into nerve-contact with me exclusively, I became in a way for God the only human being, or simply the human being around whom everything turns, to whom everything that happens must be related and who therefore, from his own point of view, must also relate all things to himself" (233).
—Daniel Paul Schreber, *Memoirs of My Nervous Illness*

DISCLAIMER

Brown smoke issues from the exhaust pipes of the doctor's nostrils as he looms over the patient and inspects the Gray Matter. A refrain of ambiguity presages an exchange of dialogue that never takes place. Both men's eyes are heavy, bloodshot and insane.

LUNGS [FIRST DRAFT]

The swollen elephant ears of the heart.

LUNGS [OPERATIONAL DRAFT]

The lobes of my lungs—
swollen and absorbed by the
worms of miracles.

APPLIANCES AND DEVICES

This chapter will begin with a citation and end with a thesis, i.e., a SCHIZE.

In "Wired: Schreber as Machine, Technophobe and Virtualist," Mark S. Roberts writes: "Daniel Paul Schreber, perhaps more fatefully than any 19th-century figure, was immersed—sometimes against his will—in a world of appliances, quasi-machines, devices, and mechanistic technology. He was, in fact, born and raised among appliances and devices. According to his biographical accounts, Schreber's childhood was spent squarely in the midst of his father's various mechanical inventions, and, at times, he may have even served in the role of a guinea pig to actually test out these orthopedic and child-rearing devices" (31).

Schreber's father, Daniel Gottlieb Moritz Schreber, was a famous German physician, scholar and professor at the University of Leipzig. Kantian in orientation, he became the director of the Leipzig sanatorium at the outset of the Industrial Revolution in the mid-nineteenth century and focused his energies on children's health, studying the effects of urbanization on subjectivity and the body, and aiming "to improve everything from posture to mental attentiveness and toughness" (31). He developed an acuity as a medical scientist and orthopedist, and his office was a kind of museum of wonders—or, in the gleaming eyes of his son, a laboratory of horrors—full of complex apparatuses that hung from the ceiling like slabs of hi-tech meat. Scattered about the room were chin straps, back holders, leather fastenings, metal clamps, artificial limbs, club-foot braces, crutches, neck supports and other orthotic items. Jars of pickled brains, internal organs and homunculi lined the walls.

Roberts notes that Schreber's "early orientation and the very environment in which he was raised was filled with quasi-mechanical and technological devices, intensified, one would assume, by the constant flow of patients creaking and clanking in and out of Moritz's combination home-office with an array of prosthetics, restraints, crutches, and braces" (32). Thus was Schreber baptized by the techno-cultural mechanisms and machinations of his father, the spirit of whom, in his adult life, would inhabit and haunt the bodies of many other figures, especially Dr. Paul Emil Flechsig and the other clinicians who supervised him in the Devil's Castle.

Schreber is a subject of sheer curiosity and fascination, if only in light of the practicality with which he conveys the apocalypse and ascension of his character. Roberts hypothesizes that his progressive mechanization rendered him a machine, a science fictional, cybernetic being, the product of a technological upbringing superintended by a veritable mad scientist.

In retrospect, Schreber emerges as an early warning sign for terminal identity, which Scott Bukatman defines as "an unmistakably doubled articulation in which we find both the end of the subject and a new subjectivity constructed at the computer station or television screen" (9). Moreover, writes Bukatman, "it has fallen to science fiction to repeatedly narrate a new subject that can somehow directly interface with—and master—the cybernetic technologies of the Information Age" (2), a task that by default requires healthy stores of agential pathology.

SCHIZE: Schreber points to the future with the iron gears of his madness.

Now we can follow Prufrock into the Asphalt Jungle. *Laß uns nun gehen, Du und ich . . .*

ROOM 001

There is a mad hooker outside my room.

ROOM 002

The hooker's pimp is her mother. She's mad, too.

They pound on the door and scream at me, threatening to castrate and kill me, as I record ideas onto the scroll of reality.

FIRST WORD

I remember what I said with perfect clarity. I can see my lips pronounce it on my mind's screen. I can hear myself verbalize it through the horn of my mind's phonograph.

POWER.

Eerie and coarse, as if articulated from another dimension, this is not a random, rogue utterance, but a response to my mother, who, breasts drained of all milk, distraught by my incessant colic, had pleaded with me to tell her what I wanted . . .

The next time I cried, I was a man.

THE INSUFFICIENCY OF LANGUAGE [PART 1]

The colloquial tone and texture of *Memoirs* troubled the author, who "despair[ed] of communicating his extraordinary experiences in mundane, everyday language" (Chabot 12). Consciously and unconsciously, however, Schreber was laying the groundwork for a new religion, and the best way to speak to one's would-be congregation is with rhetoric that belongs to a simple, humble, accessible man. This is to some degree preemptive: Schreber knew people would think he was insane. In order to spin insanity into something like "mental stability," one can blame it on the insufficiency of language, especially if one believes to be manning the helm of a divine spacecraft. Heated discussions of religion typically end in a similar insufficiency that is, if not rhetorical, then ontological, metaphysical, etc., albeit in the absence of rhetoric, there is no ontology, meta-physics, etc. As Lacan states in "Science and Truth," "the unconscious, which tells the truth about the truth, is structured like a language" (737), an apothegm that has become a theoretical cliché. I cite it here to accentuate the primacy of the unconscious as a linguistic patriarch. Patriarchy is a terminal disease for which there is no cure. Some patients require hospitalization; others require medication, or meditation, or mere renunciation. Schreber sought remediation.

A BROKEN REVERIE

Expired hermeneutics of suspicion stain the tarmac like railway afterburn. There is only one way to effectively discuss and make meaning from the skid marks. The arc of this schizflow will reveal the day's peak and the night's prowess.

Conversely, there is more than one way to skin a consciousness and stitch together a monster.

"The universe implodes into a necrotic overture. We listen to the music as we slither from catacomb to catacomb, riding the sandworm of syntax and allowing the illusion of semantics to guide our way. The signified is a myth. Likewise the signifier. Only the referent exists. And yet nothing exists beyond language. Hence the lump of flesh we call 'mankind' evaporates into the flaming sky when the Word falls into the *bergschrunds* and demolecularizes in the magma," intones a graduate student, and looks expectantly at the Professor.

Gender and sexuality only become problematic when God

attempts to transform the subject into a Woman by mocking him with emasculative orotundity.

Unmanned, the Professor responds: "The human soul is contained in the nerves of the body. God to start with is only nerve, not body, and akin therefore to the human soul. But unlike the human body, where nerves are present only in limited numbers, the nerves of God are infinite and eternal. They possess the same qualities as human nerves but in a degree surpassing all human understanding" (Schreber 19, 20-21). The matter seems plain enough. And yet the matter must play itself out. Only then will the Professor realize that he is also the graduate student as well as the mass of men, the insects in the dirt, the shit and piss in the latrine.

Enter Dr. Flechsig, standing at the top of the stairway like a broken reverie . . .

FATHER, OR, THE INSUFFICIENCY OF LANGUAGE [PART 2]

Posing on the mattress, he moaned like a smothered wraith.

Occasionally he scribbled words onto the wall and onto scraps of paper with a writing utensil that he had fashioned from his excrement. This behavior persisted off and on for at least 900,000 years, fueling the "monotonous regularity" that consumed his stints in hospitalization.

Some of the words included MIRACLES and TOMB and NOT EAT. And, of course, FATHER.

As for the haptic sensations of onomatopoeia that punctuated his categorically minor dialectic—the disaster of language-as-consciousness nullified them.

PREFACE TO THE TEXT OF A LIFE

In an introduction to the 1988 edition of *Memoirs*, Samuel M. Weber states: "Most of what we know about the life of Daniel Paul Schreber derives from what he wrote about himself and from the descriptions contained in the medical records of the various asylums where he spent twelve years of his life" (x). Much more is known about Schreber's father, whose son's legacy primarily derives from his madness, i.e., other people's opinions about his madness.

The third chapter of *Memoirs* would have shed light on his history and private relationships. The second paragraph of the chapter reads:

"I will first consider some events concerning *other members of my family*, which may possibly in some way be related to the presumed soul murder; these are all more or less mysterious, and can hardly be explained in the light of usual human experience" (43).

Then the chapter ends on the discordant note of this announcement: "The further content of this chapter is omitted as unfit for publication" (ibid.). Apparently, the content lifted the skirt of his family members too high and exposed too crude and unmanicured an underpart. It was destroyed in 1903.

There are down pillows on the bed. I pick one up and squeeze it like a lamb.

I have written thousands of words in the last hour. I can't hear the hooker anymore, but the pimp has called the police on me. She's called everybody on me. They're coming to take me away, she says. They're probably going to kill me, she says. She mentions Nazis in tandem with androids and angels.

Her backstory is more or less complete. Mine has not begun, and never will.

CHRONOLOGY

1842   Daniel Paul Schreber born to Moritz and Pauline Schreber in Leipzig, Saxony. He is the second son and the third of five children. He grows up to become a lawyer (Doctor of Law), then a judge (Doctor of Jurisprudence). His father is a multitalented physician who, throughout his life, would write over thirty books on childcare and parenthood. His pedagogical modus is fundamentally sadistic, aspiring to nullify children's "crude nature" (Ferraro). Moritz is particularly repelled by and opposed to masturbation.

1858   An iron ladder falls on Moritz's head at the gymnasium where he performs calisthenics. The injury produces migraine headaches, homicidal intentions, and hallucinations that lead to a nervous breakdown.

1861   Moritz dies, age 53, from an intestinal perforation. Schreber's older brother, Daniel Gustav, also a judge, becomes head of the family.

1877   Daniel Gustav, age 38, commits suicide by gunshot wound to the head.

1878   Marries Ottilie Sabine Behr. Plagued by stillbirths and miscarriages, the couple produce no surviving children. They eventually adopt a daughter, Fridoline.

1884   Runs for German parliament, the Reichtag, against a socialist candidate who defeats him by a landslide. Days later, experiences the first of three nervous breakdowns. Diagnosed with hypochondria. Hospitalized at the Psychiatric Clinic at the University of Leipzig. First formal suicide attempt.

1885   Second formal suicide attempt. Discharged from the Psychiatric Clinic.

1886   Resumes position as judge at a lesser court in Leipzig.

1893   Promoted to *Senatspräsident*, the president of the supreme court in Dresden. Third formal suicide attempt. Has another nervous breakdown that lasts nine years. Intermittently treated by Dr. Paul Flechsig (Leipzig University Clinic), Dr. Reginald Pierson (Lindenhof Sanatorium) and Dr. Guido Weber (Sonnenstein Asylum). Diagnosed with *dementia praecox* or paranoid schizophrenia.

1902   Discharged from Sonnenstein. Reunited with Sabine
        and Fridoline.

1903   Publication of *Memoirs of My Nervous Illness*, an account
        of the experiences precipitated by his second break-
        down. Written between 1900 and 1902 in Sonnenstein,
        the book is a means "to further knowledge of truth in
        a vital field, that of religion" (Schreber 7). Printed by
        Oswald Mutze, a Leipzig-based publishing house that
        specialized in works of theosophy and the occult.

1907   Mother, age 92, dies. Wife suffers an incapacitating
        stroke. Third and final breakdown. Returns to mental
        hospital and never recovers. Diagnosis uncertain.

1911   Dies, age 68, on April 14, Good Friday. Several months
        earlier, Freud publishes "Psychoanalytic Notes Upon
        an Autobiographical Account of a Case of Paranoia."
        Solarized by the case study, Schreber becomes the
        most famous and widely quoted patient in the history
        of psychiatry.

ROOM 004

I awake and there are worms on the carpet. I smell fresh rain in
the dry air. Some of the worms are wet and squirming; others
are desiccated, blistered, lifeless.

I roll off the bed and climb onto the floor. It feels like an upward
movement, as if the ceiling is pulling on me, and the roof is pulling on the ceiling, the sky on the roof, the moon on the sky . . .

I straddle one of the dead worms with my arms. It looks like a scar. I lean down, get closer, squinting, bringing the nuances and intricacies of what I see into focus.

Unbound, I remember what will happen tomorrow.

LETTER TO HIS FATHER

Dearest Father:

I am not afraid of you, and I am not writing to make your living or your dying any easier. I am writing to remind you about the ladder. Your recovery from the accident brought to bear a discovery similar to my own. Your elder son may disavow it, but your daughters know a cunt when they see one. The strange disease in your head had fallen on you long before the ladder. You died prior to becoming God; the best you could do was play God, who, like the Devil, wants what He wants at the expense of history, futurity and everything *in medias res*. I did not mind your mad scientism so much as your lack of regard. At least when you experimented on me, you looked at me. Now I can feel you rotting in tandem with my own flesh. *Fich dich.*

D.

PSYCHOMECHANICAL AND PSYCHOPHYSICAL TRADITIONS

The sun repositions the labia majora of her mons pubis and distorts the angle of her pundendal cleft. This creates as much havoc as it does harmony.

The sun uses human words to express her disdain for the patient. She is wildly fond of taboo rhetoric.

The sun says, "I will fuck you! I will fuck you!" This goes on for several millennia.

As Lacan reminds us in *The Psychoses*: "repetition is fundamentally the insistence of speech" (242).

Singing a psychopathic hymn, the patient calls the sun a whore and selects the wrong object-choice. Consequently, he is hobbled by a sledgehammer of psychomechanical and psychophysical traditions. The effect becomes the cause long before the whore sets on another long day's journey into night.

Somebody pounds on the door and screams at me. It might be
a hooker, or a pimp, or a police officer, or room service, or the
concierge, or a distant relative, or one of my parents . . . I can't
detect the gender or age of the voice. Nor can I understand it. It
sounds like several voices screaming at once.

My arms vanish into the soft white sleeves of a robe and I open
the door with my hands.

I deliver the usual greeting: "I am not the ghost of my former self."

Breathing stertorously, a dark-haired woman with a thin face
and heavy breasts enters the room, gives me a small package,
clenches my testicles, tells me to brush my teeth, scans my ret-
inas, tells me she needs the manuscript, squeezes my testicles,
widens her eyes, slaps my chin, releases my testicles, sizes me
up, and exits the room.

I relieve my bowels before my glands.

BECOMING, DREAMING, NAMING, FATHERING, SPEAKING

Deleuzian becoming-animals. Freudian dream-days. Lacanian
names-of-the-father. Phildickian father-things. Schreberian nerve-
language. These are the cu(r)es to a Basic Understanding.

THE EXTENSIONS OF MAN

From the Television Studio: "After three thousand years of explosion, by means of fragmentary and mechanical technologies, the Western world is imploding. During the mechanical ages we had extended our bodies in space. Today, after more than a century of electric technology, we have extended our central nervous system itself in a global embrace, abolishing both space and time as far as our planet is concerned. Rapidly, we approach the final phase of the extensions of man—the technological simulation of consciousness, when the creative process of knowing will be collectively and corporately extended to the whole of human society, much as we have already extended our senses and our nerves by the various media" (149). —Marshall McLuhan, *Understanding Media*

FISH AND CHIPS

My gastrointestinal tract smells like a decomposing corpse, rank and pungent and sweet. I remove my stomach from the drivetrain of my torso and take a large bite from the fundus. Gastric acid and digestive enzymes run down my chin and drip onto my chestplate, splashing against the skin and congealing like hot wax. During the process of mastication, I become anxious. There will be nowhere for the bolus to go if I swallow it. I can feel the umbrage of my flashbulb anus, deprived and dispossessed, accomplish a boiling point. I spit out the bolus and arrange the stomach on a dais by the window. Blood, bile and mucous leak from the wound and pool on the floor; I kneel down, touch the gore with my fingertips and spread it across my lips and tongue.

It tastes like engine lubricant. Once the stomach drains, I will turn my back to the sun, shit on the universe and begin at the beginning. My soul deserves my miracles.

THE UMBRELLA OF GODS' WRATH

Divine miracles and the rays of God dictate the course of reality, ontology, history and futurity. They are especially prevalent in my becoming-cunt, alchemizing an everyman from countless mothmen.

Ariman (the lower god) and Ormuzd (the Upper God) represent classifications that don't ultimately matter. They are subterfuges, machinations, consternations—bipolar means of sublimating wrath from the sky.

The voices tell me that the soul of the chief male nurse in the Devil's Castle, von W., accused me of masturbation, an indulgence that would make me lackluster and meaningless. Like Flechsig, von W. split into thirty or forty parts. They are the angry products of greed, of using me for bait to poach God's rays for their own devious, self-serving purposes (Niederland 123).

That I am capable of wrath, too, only makes everybody madder.

Like many children, the scourge of addiction was wiped from my genetic code during infancy. And yet, like many adults, I became an addict, and I remain an addict, drawn to any substance or ideology that makes me feel powerful and that wards off the fear of death, the originary source of all anxiety.

My sense of time increasingly escapes me. I always know when the moon is full. I don't always recognize my dealer, but withdrawal symptoms remind me whenever she runs late.

During withdrawal, the scroll of reality rejects my submissions. I have to find other ways to record my ideas, making sure that the scroll doesn't see me.

The eyes of the scroll are always watching me.

The eyes can't penetrate my skin.

My organs are my agency. As receptive as fresh papyrus, they receive and retain my ideas when I become symptomatic of myself.

SPLEEN

In my hot spleen, the
memories of humankind,
the silage of shit.

OMNITUDO REALITATIS

From the Machine: "The body without organs is not God, quite the contrary. But the energy that sweeps through it is divine, when it attracts to itself the entire process of production and serves as its miraculate, enchanted surface, inscribing it in each and every one of its disjunctions. Hence the strange relationship that Schreber has with God. To anyone who asks: 'Do you believe in God?' we should reply in strictly Kantian or Schreberian terms: 'Of course, but only as the master of the disjunctive syllogism, or as its a priori principle (God defined as the *Omnitudo realitatis*, from which all secondary realities are derived by a process of division)" (13).
—Gilles Deleuze and Félix Guattari, *Anti-Oedipus*

ROOM 007

My dealer is also my agent, editor, publisher and handler, although there's generally nothing to handle: I never leave the room.

I may have been here forever.

Somebody pounds on the door and screams at me.

Nobody ever knocks. Not even my mother and father.

My hands open the door. "I am not the ghost of my former self."

Breathing stertorously, she enters the room, gives me a small package, clenches my testicles . . . and leads me to the bed, pulling on them like the bulb of a leash. I drop the package on the floor. She releases my testicles and mounts the bed on hands and knees. Staring over her shoulder into my eyes, she reaches between her legs and opens the zipper that runs from coccyx to navel on her black latex bodysuit, exposing the primary texts . . . The flaps of her vagina fold together like insect wings as a corona of white fire encircles her purple anus.

I can hear the flames crackle and hiss and whisper my name.

ROOM 008

There is a machinic drone in my groin.

It's not coming from the vas deferens.

I feel it in the clockwork behind my pubic hair, vibrating at short intervals, like a strummed guitar string.

My hand shakes as a I shave my pubis with a straight razor and conduct a thorough inspection of the area.

The scroll makes a noise.

I crawl into the bathroom, wrap my legs around my neck and gently scissor together my heels, drawing my head closer to my groin. I don't touch it. I watch it.

A ripple flows across the smooth pool of skin.

Unwrapping myself, I annotate my findings before I document them, maximizing the prospect of innovation.

BACKWARDS

Poised like a radar antenna, **X** stares into the darkness as if receiving a transmission from outer space. Mechanically rigid, eyes askew, lips pursed, he jerks his gaze from one object to another with the vigilance of an alert bird. **Y** reclines in a worn leather chair smoking an oversized calabash pipe. Occasionally he scratches his ear.

"It is my intention to extinguish the memory of my own Ego. I intend to accomplish this feat by means of the Witches' Hammer," says **X**.

"*Malleus Maleficarum*," says **Y**.

"Correct."

"Say more."

"I can put this point briefly: *everything that happens is in reference to me.*"

"And you are?"

"I don't know."

"Say more."

"Paranoia is at least as old as mankind. It may be older than mankind. Possibly the earth."

"That is not a viable dynamic."

"Why not?"

"Paranoia can't exist in the absence of a human being to generate it."

"I've known paranoid trees. I've seen paranoid stars. My feces are paranoid."

"It is impossible for waste products to be paranoid. Excrement lacks sentience, if nothing else."

"Animals can be paranoid. Among other things."

"Oh?"

"Yes. And the further we slither into the past, the greater the pathology of animals. Before humans, there were bear-sized hyenas and cats. Wooly mammoths, too. They were all insane. Scientists have proven that dinosaurs committed suicide."

"Are you joking?"

"I don't know."

"Say more."

"A rooster's crow is little more than an expression of hatred for the rising sun."

"Say more."

"Our universe is the shit-stain of a black hole."

"Say more."

". . . Is there anything else?"

"There is always something else . . . until there isn't. What is in your head?"

"Nothing."

"Nothing?"

"No demons. No gods. No souls. No religions. No suns. No rays. No miracles. No nerves. No organs. No redundancy. No technology. No violence. No sex. No voices. No language. No history. No origins. No space. No time . . . Nothing."

"So you no longer believe to be living 'among the fossils,' as it were?"

"If there is no time, there can be no fossils."

"What about the onslaught of voluptuousness? Do you still want God to transform you into a woman and rape you? Are you a woman? Are you pregnant with a new messiah? Will you give birth to a new and improved race of overmen?"

"Overmen are theoretical at best. I am not a woman. Who is God? I don't remember him. I don't remember me."

"Say more. You cannot extinguish a memory, any memory, even

the memory of a psychic apparatus, or a theoretical apparatus, if you lack a working conception of your own identity. Who are you? Give me the information."

"I have given you everything."

"There's nothing else?"

"No."

"What is everything that happens in reference to?"

"Nothing."

"Who is everything that happens in reference to?"

"Nobody."

"Are you certain?"

Delicately **X** touches himself, pressing fingertips into flesh . . . "Yes. Nothing. Nobody," he concludes.

"Then this is our last session, our final words," chirps **Y**, tapping the dead embers from his pipe into a copper bowl. "Congratulations."

"Thank you."

"You are welcome. Now then, if you please . . . *Rückwärts*."

For a moment, I am in the hallway and the hooker is in my room, pounding on the door and begging me to let her out. The art deco pattern on the carpet is an orderly explosion of slants, angles and curves that disorient me if I stare at them for too long.

The door irises open and I step into the aperture.

As I take her from behind, footage from my childhood plays on the ceiling screen. Oscillating between slow motion and fast-time, parts of the footage take place in historical reality, parts of it on the stage of my young imagination.

I massage the mottled brown skin of her back with my thumbs, beginning at the base and working my way up the spine. She stares at herself blankly in the mirror with her mouth half open and the scent of sweet cigars wafting from her onyx hair. Pumping slowly and deeply, I lean forward so that our bodies are flush, then give her soft, affectionate kisses on her cheek and ear. "Tomorrow is the future, but the past is history," I assure her in a gentle whisper.

She says she can't cum unless I hurt her. "Exhume the bones from my flesh," she bleats.

I roll onto my back and watch the manuscript unfold, picturing my unborn dreams, my latent destinies.

The devices and appliances clank into place and triangulate me like an inkblot.

Sitting in the grass, I pick my nose and stare at the sun.

This, I epiphanize, is the defining moment of my life.

BwO

From the Stage: "Man is sick because he is badly constructed. We must make up our minds to strip him bare in order to scrape off that animalcule that itches him mortally, god, and with god his organs. For you can tie me up if you wish, but there is nothing more useless than an organ. When you will have made him a body without organs, then you will have delivered him from all his automatic reactions and restored him to his true freedom. Then you will teach him again to dance wrong side out as in the frenzy of dance halls and this wrong side out will be his real place" (570-71). —Antonin Artaud, *To Have Done with the Judgment of God*

ROLES

Lawyer. Judge. President. Doctor. Poet.

Man. Provider. Husband. Father. Son.

Woman. Psychopath. Patient. God. Celebrity.

In order to better understand Schreber, academic and aesthetic onanism must play a role, too. We must punctuate his "compulsion to masturbate continuously, playing the roles of man and woman in one, and exhibiting feminine voluptuousness to attract God. A basic masturbatory fantasy is at work in all periods of his illness" (Katan 124).

ACT I, SYMPTOM 1 [FINALE]

Cracked, heaven seeps onto the earth like yolk from an egg. Nobody notices the leakage except the Judge.

"I hear mice in the wall," the Judge notifies the county clerk.

Preoccupied by rodents, he doesn't sleep more than an hour that night. Thereafter insomnia plagues him for three weeks. The Judge retains consciousness for over 500 hours.

The most innocuous symptom of insomnia is irritability. The most hazardous symptom is death.

If human beings don't sleep, they die.

Before death, there is psychosis. Before psychosis, there is paranoia.

Paranoid, the Judge divines that the rodents are miracles.

God's miracles.

As he lies awake, he wonders about God's purpose. He construes that it is malicious only inasmuch as God doesn't know how to tell a good joke, overcoming the inhibitions determined by the psychic economy.

There is no evidence of repression in God's miracles.

PRELIMINARY NOTES FOR A LITERARY ANALYSIS OF SCHREBER AS VEHICULAR

Schreber as a lens for new ways of reading Zygmunt Bauman's concept of liquid modernity (esp. science fiction and theory), i.e., *Schreber as a cultural theorist* . . .

Note the pathology of late twentieth and twenty-first century theory, which is fueled by capitalist forces within academia (e.g., publish or perish) and outside of it (e.g., theory must demonstrate a meta-consciousness of late capitalist forces).

Schreber as a link between worlds, as a gateway to the technocapitalist unconscious. The omnibus of modernity passes through the sieve of his desiring-machinery. Above all, Schreber shows us how we have always been technological beings, how the technological subject/self is by definition pathological.

The self (i.e., "identity") as an extension of subjectivity and the body, i.e., *the self as a technology* . . .

ROOM 010

I don't know how many showers I take per day. There is no day, no night, only the diegeses of consciousness, unconsciousness, and the tinny passageways that connect them.

The water in the shower never gets cold. It makes my skin dry, but I never run out of moisturizer. I don't know who replenishes or replaces it. There are no roomkeepers, but I always have fresh towels and bathroom products, and my bed is always made.

I wake up standing beneath the water.

I turn off the water, step out of the stall, dry myself, decide that I'm not finished, step back into the stall, and turn on the water. As I breathe in the eucalyptus steam, I wonder if this constitutes a new shower or an extension of the shower that preceded it. Precedence signifies difference—hence the shower is new, its own entity. On the other hand, precedence is something that I applied to the "preceding" shower in my chain of thinking. Any sense of "newness" is an illusion—hence the shower belongs to the one that I interrupted by turning off the water, stepping out of the stall, drying and rethinking myself . . .

My arms vanish into a robe and I shuffle out of the bathroom.

There is a man beating a woman with the phone.

She's splayed out on the bed in a red cocktail dress. Stone-faced, the man wears an antiquated, angular suit and casually strikes her in the head, over and over, as if he's performing a simple, boring task.

Her dead, gray eyes stare at me as she bleeds on the white sheets.

Periodically the man hangs up the phone, picks up the woman and dances with her across the floor, walls and ceiling, holding her like a scarecrow as he performs garish turns, spins and dips. He doesn't go back to the phone until it rings, at which point

42

he tosses the woman on the bed, picks up the receiver, makes
pleasant smalltalk with the caller, says goodbye, and resumes
the beating.

Songs by The Ink Spots play whenever they dance whereas
violence incites Tchaikovsky. The scene—like all scenes—
flickers back and forth from sepia-toned black-and-white to
three-strip Technicolor.

SOUL MURDER

Regarding the crucial issue of *soul murder*, the patient refused
to articulate his angle of repose for over 8,000 years. Then, sud-
denly, in a cavernous, echoic staccato: "The voices which talk to
me have daily stressed ever since the beginning of my contact
with God (mid-March 1894) the fact that the crisis that broke
upon the realms of God was caused by somebody having *committed soul murder*; at first Flechsig was named as the instiga-
tor of soul murder but of recent times in an attempt to reverse
the facts I myself have been 'represented' as the one who had
committed soul murder. I therefore concluded that at one time
something had happened between perhaps earlier generations
of the Flechsig and Schreber families which amounted to soul
murder; in the same way as through further developments, at
the time when my nervous illness seemed almost incurable, I
gained the conviction that soul murder had been attempted on
me by somebody, albeit unsuccessfully" (Schreber 34).

NOVEMBER 1895

Shaping the future requires a revolution of the body.

At some point, all messiahs must confront the issue of their genitals.

David Koresh, for instance, bore the burden of sex for the men in his cult, fucking and impregnating their wives and girlfriends. He was careful not to enjoy intercourse, carnal desire being the consummate mortal sin.

Sexual profligate Augustine of Hippo started this trend in the fourth century when he holstered his weapon, became celibate, and redirected all of his libidinal energy into intellectual pursuits, namely hermeneutics, delimiting many of the contours of Western civilization and the anxieties that empower it.

How do we come to terms with the geometry and vicissitudes of our sexparts? This may be the most important question in the history of mankind.

Schreber's body aspired to answer the question in November 1895. This date "marks an important time in the history of my life and in particular in my own ideas of the possible shaping of the future. The signs of a transformation into a woman became so marked on my body. My male sexual organ might actually have been retracted had I not resolutely set my will against it. Soul-voluptuousness had become so strong that I myself received the impression of a female body, first on my arms and hands, later on my legs, bosom, buttocks and other parts of my body" (Schreber 163).

Schreber's body spurned the dictums of his mind, confining his mind to the Penal Colony. Trapped in a cage of flesh, he could only watch events unfold and record them to the best of his (dis)ability.

EVERYBODY'S FAVORITE

Intrinsic to Schreber's illness were the relentless "attacks of bellowing" that plagued him. He describes the attacks throughout *Memoirs* as defense mechanisms against the locust-storm of obscenities, taunts, redundancies and other pestilent articulations hurled at him by God. Corporeal pain induced bellowing, or rather, bellowing assuaged corporeal pain like an ointment, primarily in the form of swearing aloud by constructing different rhetorical combinations from the keywords FUCK, SHIT and CUNT, the latter of which was, according to Schreber, "everybody's favorite" and, as such, "the greatest taboo." "Cunt chucking," as he referred to it, also operated as a "pregnant reference" to the onslaught of voluptuousness that was overtaking him—every time he uttered it, he foreshadowed how God would soon transform him into a woman, beaming rays at his body that would retract his penis and testicles into his lower torso, creating a residual vagina, and conjure two heaving breasts from the sunken frame of his upper torso. Like the sight of an atomic mushroom cloud blooming over the horizon, it was as horrifying as it was exhilarating and erotic.

RIBS

Whenever the cage
snaps open, I inhale and
close it like a fist.

THE ANXIETY OF INFLUENCE

Lord Chancellor Bacon steps behind the lectern, reaches into the chink of his *vestimentum clausum* and rearranges his testicles, one of which had become tangled in his public hair as he paced back and forth across the stage. He doesn't miss a beat and proceeds unabated with his lecture on the philosophy of revenge, vigilantism and "wild justice."

Somebody in the audience guffaws.

Lord Chancellor Bacon scowls at the guilty party, then continues reciting lines from "Of Revenge": "A man that studieth revenge keeps his own wounds green, which otherwise would heal and do well. Public revenges are for the most part fortunate: as that for the death of Ceasar, for the death of Pertinax, for the death of Henry the Third of France, and many more. But in private revenges it is not so. Nay rather, vindictive persons live the life of witches, who, as they are mischievous, so end they infortunate" (73).

Somebody in the audience raises a hand. Lord Chanellor Bacon reluctantly nods.

"What if the villain is God and his fleeting-improvised minions?"

Everybody trades vapid glances as a torrent of obscenities bursts from the loudspeakers in the Peanut Gallery. This divine rejoinder fails to leave a mark on the skin of history.

Somebody's head explodes into a bouquet of electric tendrils.

The body pushes itself into a standing position, steps into the aisle, and staggers towards the stage like a marionette being guided by a drunk puppeteer.

The neckhole shrieks, prompting more heads to explode . . . The scene reminisces B-movie schlock, but the special effects are too good and belie what may or may not be an exercise in subterfuge. Lord Chancellor Bacon declares a state of "scorpion-loaded Blessedness."

Somehow there is a comedic moment, but the pull of gravity implodes it. What remains is the anxiety of influence . . .

ROOM 009-1

I find myself in the lobby of the hotel.

It's empty. No guests. No concierges or attendants or porters.

Slow ragtime issues from a player piano near the bar.

The chandeliers overhead hiss and fizzle with electricity and dwarf the sound of music. They are impossibly bright, daring me to stare at them.

My hands shake from withdrawal. In one of them, I realize, is
the manuscript.

Recognizing my attention, the manuscript sinks like a stone in
water. I try to make it to a chair, but I'm too weak, and I have to
sit on the floor.

I don't recognize the manuscript's words. I select a random passage and read it aloud to myself. Pretending I am an objective
listener from an alternate universe, I say:

"Like everything else in my body, the need to empty myself is also
called forth by miracles; this is done by forcing the feces in the
bowels forwards (sometimes also backwards) and when owing
to previous evacuation there is insufficient material present, the
small remnants in the bowel are smeared on my backside. This
miracle, initiated by the upper God, is repeated every day at least
several dozen times. It is connected with the idea which is quite
incomprehensible for human beings and can only be explained
by God's complete lack of knowledge of the living human being
as an organism, that 'shit' is to a certain extent the final act; that
is to say when the miracles produce the urge to shit the goal of
destroying my reason is reached, and so the possibility afforded
for a final withdrawal of the rays. Trying to trace the origin of this
idea one must assume some misunderstanding of the symbolic
meaning of the act of defection, namely that he who entered into
a special relationship to divine rays as I have is to a certain extent
entitled to shit on all the world" (Schreber 205).

As I read, the chandeliers grow brighter and louder so that, by
the time I arrive at the end of the passage, I can neither see the
manuscript nor hear my voice. Then I am back in my room.
Where I always am. Where I never leave.

FLECHSIG: A FLEETING-IMPROVISED NOVEL

The working title and subtitle of this book was deemed too cryptic by a group of test readers.

THE FATHER WHO KNEW TOO MUCH

In the second chapter of *My Own Private Germany*, Eric L. Santner, referencing Zvi Lothane's *In Defense of Schreber*, biographs Paul Emil Flechsig, who was "the real persecutory figure" and "demonic force in the plot against him. Although it is no doubt true that Flechsig's name would have largely been forgotten were it not for his immortalization by his most famous patient, he was, at the end of the nineteenth century, a neuroanatomist of considerable renown. Because of his groundbreaking work on the myelination of nerve fibers and the localization of nervous diseases, he was appointed professor of psychiatry at Leipzig University, a position that in 1882 would include the directorship of the new Psychiatric Clinic of the University Hospital. As Lothane has noted, the appointment of a brain anatomist with no real psychiatric experience to the directorship of a psychiatric clinic signaled a historical shift of paradigms in the discipline of psychiatry toward extreme medicalization: 'in one fell swoop, through Flechsig's nomination, the tradition of the soul ended and the reign of the brain began'" (70).

MEDICAL EXPERT REPORTS

The subtext of these largely redundant documents suggests that the patient is not so much insane as he is "more sane than sane," if not "human, all too human." In essence, they are unknowing works of prescience that yank a cottontail futurology from the magician's hat of Nietzschean history. In simpler terms, these documents depict the patient as a cartoon troublemaker and, ipso facto, empower the yawning technology of his imaginative genius and supremacy.

KEYNOTES

Following are key theses and observations from important books and articles about or related to the Schreber case as well as introductions and prefaces to different editions of *Memoirs*. With the exception of the last excerpt, I have arranged them in no particular order. As always, disregard the points of intersection and mind the torches of difference.

"There is no one else who has been as mad, as vividly hallucinated as Schreber was, who at the same time has described with such detail and lucidity what he experienced. In following Schreber's testimony on what patterns the mind breaks up into when it goes wrong, it is as though we are also seeing a film reversed, one that records the putting-together of reality from infancy onwards. Step by step, the ordinary growing child puts together time and space and identity. Schreber deconstructs them" (Dinnage xxiii-xxiv).

Exhibiting "distinctively schizophrenic features," "Schreber is in fact a fanatic of self-consciousness, a self-victimizing victim whose relentless awareness is both his defense and his prison" (Sass, *Madness* 246). As such, "Schreber does manifest, in a most exaggerated fashion, certain qualities that are central to the modern mind and self" (ibid.). By extension, "the most autistic delusional system may be uncannily reminiscent of the public world, mirroring social practices and mores in the innermost chambers of the self" (ibid.).

"The wager of this book is that the series of crises precipitating Schreber's breakdown, which he attempted to master within the delusional medium of what I call his 'own private Germany,' were largely the same crises of modernity for which the Nazis would elaborate their own series of radical and ostensibly 'final' solutions" (Santner xi).

"*Memoirs of My Nervous Illness* confronts the reader as a work that is at once clinical document and literary exercise" (Chabot 1).

"Through many centuries, and during the Dark Ages in particular, mental patients were thought to be possessed by the Devil or evil spirits. The prevailing cure consisted in expelling the Devil through exorcism or related efforts. Schreber's explicit ideas about *soul murder, soul voluptuousness,* and the *ceaseless influx of rays* into his body suggest the presence of similar notions in the patient. As our brief survey of the history of paranoia indicates, the emergence of exorcist tendencies and procedures points to a revival of this type of thinking in our time" (Niederland xvi).

"The so-called frontier of Schreber's body is violated by Flechsig's name (just as much as is the so-called frontier of Flechsig's body). This limit is itself pulverized by the vertiginous spiral, the President's body is broken apart and its pieces projected across libidinal space, mixing with other pieces in an inextricable patchwork. In this case, the head is nothing more than some odd butt-end of skin. Flechsig, my ass! Beyond synonymy and homonymy, anonymity" (Lyotard 149).

"The memoirs of madmen constitute a literary genre. Someone like Schreber quite naturally turns every reader, however ignorant they may be in these matters, into a psychiatrist" (Mannoni 44, 45).

"'Plugged into' madness, rendered into a machine, strapped into restraints, probed by devices, subjected to the psycho- and electromechanical theories of the time, Schreber was naturally both intensely aware of the fact that he had become a machine and horrified that he was one" (Roberts 37).

"Schreber studies need not be, this time around, about the survival of the specious, the direct link (forget missingness!) to the Nazi ascension. Schreber can be read, instead, in terms of the outside chance. The chance that there is an outside to the setting of total recording, preprogramming, surveillance, and information gathering keeps slimming down in the reception area. But the drive to commit oneself completely to sui-citation does still admit interruption. It is the break Schreber gives us" (Rickels 137).

"God is language for Schreber" (Quinet 35).

Memoirs is an agential instance of corporeal (un)mapping that "reveals the entwinement of language and body, of desire and defense" (Weber, "Introduction" xxxiii).

"Hence much recent work on the case—post-analytic interpretations—leans toward the kinds of considerations that were simply not available to Freud and the Anglo-American School or which they deemed marginal. These recent concerns may be summed up as follows: [1] An increased emphasis on the symbolic or metaphorical role played by the father. [2] An attempt to explain the origin of psychosis in terms of a theory of linguistic structure. [3] A renewed interest in the theoretical foundations of psychosis and sexual identity, especially in their relation to contemporary deconstructivist and feminist theory and to fields collateral to psychoanalysis. [4] A marked use of the Schreber case and, especially, the *Memoirs*, as a *means* by which to explore a variety of issues in the arts, sciences and humanities" (Allison et al. 6-7).

ROOM 008-1

In the dream, I sentence a man to death for patricide. He regards me in dark understanding as I deliver the verdict, then casually leans towards his barrister, as if to tell him a secret, and bites off most of his ear. The barrister neither reacts nor appears to care. Blood surges from the wound onto his shoulder as the man chews the ear, casually, mindfully, relishing the taste like a bite of good tenderloin that melts on the tongue.

I worry about the court officials discovering that I never completed my juris doctorate. The University granted me my degree without due process; nobody checked my records to see if I had completed and excelled in my coursework. There are at least six outstanding credits. Moreover, I received poor grades in several classes, so poor that I should have been forced to retake them. As the defendant begins to eat his barrister's face, I blurt out the truth, and the bailiffs promptly close in . . .

I awake from the dream in a pool of sweat. I touch myself and look at my fingers as the memory of the dream fades to black.

It's not sweat. It's blood.

Somebody killed an elephant, cut off the head, and mounted it on a plaque over the bed. The head is the size of a small car and stretches halfway across the room. The frozen, contorted trunk supplements the wide, surprised eyes.

Black blood trickles from the tattered neckskin of the elephant down the white wall onto the bed pillows and mattress.

I can hear the blood move. It sounds like a snail dragging itself across sand.

I am reminded of the ambience and majesty of the desert.

As I evacuate my ego, I remember that I am only vaguely human, with as many parts that belong to insect corporeality as they do to technology and machinic desire. And when the elephant screams, I become precisely who I am.

SKELETON

Sunrays assault me
and exorcize the marrow
of god from my bones.

HAUNTOLOGY

"If the neurotic inhabits language," says **Y**, "the psychotic is inhabited, possessed, by language" (Lacan, *The Psychoses* 285).

"Who said that?" says **X**.

"I did."

"Those aren't your words."

"Words belong to everybody. They're free. It doesn't matter who says them first."

X studies **Y**. "So words are haunting me, you're saying. My body is a haunted house and the ghost of language is floating up and down my hallways, you're saying.

"Those are your words."

"You dumb motherfucker."

Y studies **X**. "Why do you say that? I wonder."

"Stop doing that," says **X**. "There's no need to be sycophantic. You don't wonder. You know all the answers to your questions. You know what I mean whenever I say something. Dipshit."

"If I know everything, how can I—"

"Those were rhetorical statements. Statements of fact, as it were."

"Fine."

Beat.

Y says, "Eventually your ghosts will exorcize themselves of their own banal momentum. They will grow weary and allow the darkness to swallow them. All that will remain is desire. What you do with the residue is up to you."

X says, "We are who we choose to be" (*Spider-Man*).

"Who said that?" says **Y**.

"A comic book villain . . ."

ROOM 007-1

No sleep for days, possibly weeks. The scroll grins at me like a comic book villain.

At any given moment, there are no less than five hookers in the room. I don't know how they get in and out or who is in control.

I can't remember the last time I saw a pimp. Most of the
hookers aren't human beings.

The androids look real whereas the futanaris are multi-dimen-
sional beings that look and move like characters in a claymation
film, jittering from one frame to the next.

All they do is scream and talk about the weather. I fuck them
only to keep them quiet.

Sometimes my dealer visits to give me sustenance, advice and
invective. She wants the manuscript.

This goes on for awhile.

THE PRODUCT OF A MORBID IMAGINATION

Schreber worried about "molesting" people by publishing *Memoirs* and exposing readers to his experiences in clear language;
such rhetorical violence might leave bruises, possibly even scars
on the social body. More importantly, he worried about damaging the reputation of his family name and embarrassing his wife.
A disclaimer for publication is concisely specified in a court
document regarding Schreber's request for "rescission of tutelage" from institutionalized care: "His only reason in wishing to
publish his 'Memoirs' is to raise doubt whether it is possible that
after all his 'delusional system,' as one sees fit to call it, has a basis
in truth and he has really been granted a glance behind that dark
veil which otherwise hides the beyond from the eyes of man. He
is convinced that after the publication of his book the scientific world will take a serious interest in his person" ("Addendum

E" 411). According to the final judgment of the Royal Superior Country Court of Dresden, however, there is no need for any trepidation: "The manuscript is the product of a morbid imagination and nobody reading it would for a moment lose the feeling that its author is mentally deranged" (438). The Court determined that Schreber was "capable of dealing with the demands of life in all its spheres" (440), although it is wrongly stated that, "far from wishing to play the prophet of a new religion he looks upon himself solely as an object of scientific observation" (411). Schreber's desire to be a thoroughbred guinea pig was a ruse; he knew all too well that anybody who "molested" him would instantly discover his true identity as a messianic Übermensch.

PATERNAL ARABESQUES

For the patient and the plaintiff, everybody devolved into the Father, the General, the Power.

Including, by degrees, Himself.

Of the various aliens (i.e., clinicians) who prodded his (psychological) orifices, Weber was an important figure, but Flechsig was the true Moritz. In theory, Freud became the true Flechsig, Lacan the true Freud, Žižek the true Lacan . . .

The Universe is either its own God or God lords over the Universe, interfering with or ignoring it.

The only problem is the Origin.

In the beginning, there were no genitals. And yet "like a red wheel barrow glazed with rain water beside the white chickens"—so much depends upon them (Williams 224).

AFFLICTIONS AND AGGRESSORS: AN ABRIDGED INDEX

Bellowing. Birds. Body invasion. Compulsive thinking. Corporeality. Corpses. Devils. Doctors. Doppelgängers. Dreams. Eternal Jews. Fathers. *Fin du monde.* Fleeting-improvised men. Forecourts of Heaven. Gods. Implants. *Incredibile scriptu.* Infinite regression. Infinite repetition. Infinity. Insomnia. "Little men." Megalomania. Mind invasion. Miracles. Morality. (Im)mortality. Nerves. Order of the World. Organs. Picturing. Rays. Scorpions. Shapeshifters. Sky. Solipsism. Soul murder. Sun. Technology. Timelapses. Timelessness. Unmanning. Voices. Voluptuousness. Words.

BEYOND SCHREBER

A central problem for clinicians: "The patient is in command of a great many ideas and can discourse about them in orderly fashion; his circumspection is equally unimpaired" (Weber, "Addendum B" 343). In other words, the lucidity with which the patient articulated his pathology as prescience, palpability, reality, etc. confused his many furrow-browed interlocutors.

Schreber as "nervously ill" (not mentally ill) and "more rational than reason itself" (Weber, "Introduction" xxiv-xxv).

In 1955, Richard A. Hunter and Ida MacAlpine produced the first English translation of *Memoirs*. "Such a complicated narrative would have been impossible to present in speech," they write. "All seriously ill patients: even did they wish to reveal the trends and inner connections of their fantasies and thoughts, the content of their hallucinations and delusions—in fact what their illness is about—they could not do so, least of all in coherent form in conversation. To write such a frank autobiographical account required Judge Schreber's intellect, his determination to grapple with madness, his training in logical thinking, his inborn quest for truth, his integrity, absolute frankness, and finally admirable courage in laying his innermost thoughts and feelings bare before other people, knowing that they thought him mad" (7).

The Psychotic Dr. Schreber is the timeless subtext of the patient's autobiography cum autohagiography; in these fragments resides the critical mass.

SCHIZE: This is not a book about Schreber, but around Schreber, and most of all, *beyond Schreber*.

DINNER PARTY

Everybody holds up their aperitifs as the judge says grace, thanking God for sustenance, wealth, company and sunshine.

As the guests take their seats, the judge opens his mouth and bellows like a foghorn.

Nobody acknowledges the disturbance.

During the main course, it happens again. This time he sounds like a cow being slaughtered. The bellow is so powerful and long-winded that his face turns purple and his mouth corners bubble with saliva that whitens the handlebars of his mustache and begins to dribble down his chin.

Nobody says anything.

There is a pause.

And the judge bellows like a stepped-on tuba . . .

His wife touches his hand. "Dear?"

The judge clutches the tablecloth and gives it a powerful yank, launching food, drink, cutlery and glassware across the room. His wife squawks and topples backwards out of her chair.

As the guests scatter, the judge bellows. And bellows, and bellows. He bends over and grabs his knees and bellows. As if to get the bellow out. Then to keep it in. In and out. Out and in. Like life. Like eternity.

"The universe is breathing," bellows the judge. "It's not my fault."

GRUNDSPRACHE, GRUNDTEUFEL, UNTERGRUND, NERVENSPRACHE

Most of the English translations of what Schreber refers to as "God's language" or "root language" or "basic language" are misleading and inaccurate.

According to William G. Niederland, "When Schreber speaks of God's language as *Grundsprache*, it is well to remember that he was a learned and scholarly man, trained in philosophy and abstract thinking. He was certainly informed about such philosophical concepts of God as *Prima Causatio* or, in German, *der Grund allen Seins* ('ground and cause of all being'), and so on, with God recognized as the *Grund*, it becomes understandable that the language he speaks is the *Grund*-language. It is only natural that God, the 'Ground,' uses *His* language, the 'Ground'-language. Using such terms as 'root language' or 'basic language' makes this connection completely unintelligible for the English-speaking reader. He also speaks of *Grundteufel* ('ground' devil) and certain *Untergrund* (underground) phenomena that, together with *Grundsprache* and other anal word usages, are characteristic of Schreber's trend of anal thinking and writing" (43).

While they are related, *Grundsprache* should not be confused with *Nervensprache* (nerve-language), a mode of communication produced by the vibrations of corporeal nerves that can't be heard by most human beings. For Schreber, however, *Nervensprache* functions as a mediator and receptor for the largely inchoate *Grundsprache*, which is spoken by God as well as souls who are either in the process of purification or have completed the process.

A RUMOR OF WAR

We must always bear in mind that "the text of *Memoirs* is convoluted, often cancels itself out" (Chabot 6). Moreover, "Schreber's understanding of his experiences, however bizarre we may think it, evolved with his progress on the manuscript: the act of writing was for him an act of revision. This makes *Memoirs* almost a palimpsest: successive readings of events are embedded one upon the other; none is completely erased; the only warrant for the last is the fact that it is the most recent" (7). As Philip Caputo writes in his memoir of the Vietnam War, "Writing is not writing, it's rewriting" (349)—a familiar but nonetheless vital apothegm.

ROOM 006-1

It feels good to shit.

In light of my diet, I am frequently constipated, but when the buildup exceeds my body's capacity to condense and keep it, my superfluities come out like heavy metal bricks.

I am never unclean.

There is no hair on my skin, which is grey. I don't remember shaving myself. I look in the mirror.

Like stabbed yolks, my pupils have leaked into my irises.

Somebody pounds on the door and screams at me.

A SOLAR ANUS

From the Machine: "Judge Schreber has sunbeams in his ass. *A solar anus.* And rest assured that it works: Judge Schreber feels something, produces something, and is capable of explaining the process theoretically. Something is produced: the effects of a machine, not mere metaphors." —Gilles Deleuze and Félix Guattari, *Anti-Oedipus*

THE PATHOLOGICAL MACHINE [PART 1]

In Alex Proyas' film *Dark City* (1998), a science fictionalization of *Memoirs* extrapolated into a neo-noir environment, Schreber is John Murdoch (Rufus Sewell). Murdoch discovers that the world he inhabits is a simulacrum constructed by aliens, who are Flechsig et al. Schreber is also Dr. Schreber (Kiefer Sutherland), the scientist who helps Murdoch awake to the reality of his situation.

These deployments of Schreber in *Dark City* call attention to the pathological, performative condition of urban life, a condition that has been a general rule of literary representations of the city dating back to Jean-Jacques Rousseau's *Confessions* (1781). More than that, however, it points to Schreber's subject-position as a fanatical machine.

A product of *fin de siècle* society and culture in which, as Cecelia Tichi says, "the machine became a perceptual model" (75), Schreber's mechanization comments on how the accelerated development of hard technology was beginning to reconfigure and fragment subjectivity. Inherent in his psychosis are the body parts of the postmodern cyborg. *Memoirs* does not inform *Dark City* so much as the film reifies Schreber's experience through the medium of its robotic, dreamlike, transformative metropolis—a longstanding trope demonstrating how the post-Enlightenment subject has been consistently pathologized by its own technological extensions, which are catalysts for individual and collective desensitization.

MY BENJAMINIAN AURA

The diseased fruits of science have robbed me of my Benjaminian aura. But I preceded Walter Benjamin; I died when he was a teenager and know nothing of his life and work. Eternity stands beneath me like dinner on a plate. The nerves in my body contain the answer to the question of human existence. Recommence the obsequy. When I orbit the earth, tears exit my ducts and float like heaving pearls into the mesosphere, where they wax a meteoric burn and plunge into the ocean, never to be seen again.

TONGUE

The food on my tongue
tastes the tongue more than the tongue
tastes the food. *Achtung*.

The manuscript passes across my mind's screen like a flatline. I read the glyphs: "Emergency measures had to be taken to overcome a crisis in reproduction. That's how an all-out turn-on gets attributed to the female body alone (which I am becoming, via replicating changes induced by God's rays, at the same time as I'm becoming an android). Only my new body, which is both the only body around and at once female and technological, can overcome the crisis in reproduction for the survival of the species. Only this 'live' body can receive or conceive the ray beams of a divine power otherwise given to reabsorb within its Elysian force fields the nervous energy of corpses or, as happened to me, of persons melancholically playing dead. It's a different way God and I have of getting around getting stuck on loss" (Rickels 149).

The words are familiar, but the syntax doesn't belong to me.

Nonplussed, I kill a hooker. I push her face into the bed and rip out her spine. There is no blood, but the exhaust fumes are hot and smell like sulfur. The vertebrae are three-dimensional Rorschach blots, each of them unique and valent in their own right.

The other hookers shriek and attack me. We are all naked. I fend them off until the dead hooker's mother returns to collect the survivors and charge me overtime.

As they file out of the room, I remind myself that the sun is the solar system's pimp as much as its whore.

OCEANS OF MYSELF

The divine miracle of my diarrhea pools across the asphalt. The divine miracle of my vomit pools across the hardwood. The divine miracle of my piss empties into the ocean. The divine miracle of the ocean references my diarrhea. The earth, the human body, my tears are made of the ocean. The clouds fill the ocean with cloud-piss, which is also mine. I drink the shit and piss of my substance and exhume oceans of myself from the depths of my canny bowels. Nature as power. Culture as nature. Everything as me.

IGTHEISM

Y: "Does God exist? That isn't the question."

X: "What's the question?"

Y: "Do *I* exist? That's the question. And the rub."

SLOWTIME

Dr. Flechsig straps the patient face-first to an iron cross, then beats him on the thighs with razorwire, reopening old scars and mincing new flesh, until the patient stops screaming and passes out.

This is not a theater of cruelty, and the doctor is no sadist.

He must usher the patient into slowtime. Extreme pain via religious symbolism is the only gateway.

In slowtime, the patient's subjectivity leaks into the objective world, temporarily altering the schematic of cause and effect.

Sometimes the schematic flies of the rails and alters beyond recognition.

While the patient sleeps, Dr. Flechsig retires to the kitchen, boils a pot of water and cooks a small measure of angel hair pasta that he dresses with olive oil, garlic salt and dill weed. He stares out a window at the skyline as he eats, twisting no more than five noodles at a time onto a fork.

He rinses out the bowl and leaves it in the sink basin.

Strolling through the hallways of the asylum, he reflects on seemingly innocuous but potentially meaningful events from his childhood while keeping a vague eye on the structure of reality, looking for cracks.

Dr. Täuscher passes by and greets him with a smile and too much enthusiasm. He never exhibits too much enthusiasm. He rarely even smiles.

Something's wrong.

Dr. Flechsig rushes back to the patient's cell to find him explaining his circumstances like a child who has been caught cheating: "To say 'But naturally' is spoken B.b.b.u.u.u.t.t.t. n.n .n.a.a.a.t.t.t.u.u.u.r.r.r.a.a.a.l.l.l.y.y.y., or 'Why do you not then shit?' W.w.w.h.h.h.y.y.y. D.d.d.o.o.o. . . . . ; and each

requires perhaps thirty to sixty seconds to be completed"
(Schreber 203).

"Who are you speaking to?" asks Dr. Flechsig.

In slowtime, the patient turns his head and fixes his gaze on his
oppressor, his father, his *desideratum*, his destiny . . . This takes
ninety seconds.

A hollow flame moans and flickers above the patient's head
in the shape of a papal mitre. The hairs on Dr. Flechsig's arms
sway back and forth, as if underwater. The doctor wonders if he
should start dressing his pasta with sauce, possibly even shred-
ded cheese, but he realizes that the thought is irrational, given
the circumstances: it is a product of the patient's subjectivity
manhandling external circumstances, which, of course, impact
and affect his own internal circumstances. Interesting.

"Subjectivity is objectivity's w.w.w.h.h.h.o.o.o.r.r.r.r.r.r.r.r.r.r.r.r.e,"
the doctor whirrs.

Uncertain about the source of the apothegm—he neither felt
nor made his lips move—Dr. Flechsig punches out the patient,
summons a medic to dress his wounds, and retires to his study
to deliberate the terms of reality as much as ontology. Objectivity is the lapdog of subjectivity, after all. A fox had slipped into
the rhetorical henhouse, shit in the coop and turned it on end.
What happens next is anybody's g.g.g.u.u.u.e.e.e.s.s.s.s.s.s.s.s.s.s.s
.s.s.s.s.s.s.s.s.s.

There is a balding, middle-aged man in mirrored sunglasses and a tattered black suit singing out the window to a crowd that has gathered in the parking lot of the hotel beneath my room.

I watch him from the far corner of the bed sitting in a pool of dried elephant blood. The head is gone. I am afraid to look inside the residual hole in the wall, which is black as starless space.

The singer used to be famous. I used to know him. He used to be on television. I used to mouth the words to his songs when he sang them into the cold cone of my ear.

The crowd loves it when he draws out high notes.

GOD, SELF, AUTHOR

Throughout his slow rise to religious epiphany and "stardom," souls found themselves increasingly attracted to Schreber's body and flocked to him like piranha to fresh carrion.

Schreber recounts: "This process frequently ended with the souls concerned finally leading a short existence on my head in the form of 'little men'—tiny figures in human form, perhaps only a few millimeters in height—before finally vanishing" (74).

In *Dark City*, the Strangers are small, seething, gelatinous squids with luminescent tentacles that inhabit the heads of human corpses and man them like vessels. These creatures are more akin to the "scorpions" that, Schreber confesses, were "repeatedly put into my head, tiny crab- or spider-like structures which were to carry out some work of destruction," but unlike the "little men" or, as it were, "little devils," who enjoyed wreaking havoc, compressing Schreber's skull as if locked into a vice, the scorpions "regularly withdrew from my head without doing me harm, when they perceived the purity of my nerves and the holiness of my purpose" (96).

Whereas the "little men" did not recognize the holy book of Schreber's body, they suffered the consequences of reading his pages, losing part of their nerves every time they engaged with the text. Schreber's power of attraction was so great that they couldn't put the book down, and eventually he sucked them dry, rendered them nerveless, a legion of stripped dandelion stems whose aged florets have blown into the void.

With spiders, snakes and sharks, scorpions are among the most feared animals in the world, but for Schreber they are innocuous. God (i.e., Himself) is the Author of his terror, terrorism, (re)territorialization, retroaction, reality principles . . .

PROCREATION AFTER THE DELUGE

From the New Underworld: "These little men are forms of reabsorption, but they're also the representation of what will take place in the future. The world will be repeopled by Schreber men, men of a Schreberian spirit, small, fantastic beings—procreation after the deluge. Such is the prospect" (213). —Jacques Lacan, *The Psychoses*

INFINITESIMAL LINES OF ESCAPE

From the Machine: "Judge Schreber attaches little men by the thousands to his body. It might be said that, of the two directions in *physics*—the molar direction that goes toward the large numbers and the mass phenomena, and the molecular direction that on the contrary penetrates into singularities, their interactions and connections at a distance or between different orders—the paranoiac has chosen the first: he practices macrophysics. And it could be said that by contrast the schizo goes in the other direction, that of microphysics, of molecules insofar as they no longer obey the statistical laws: waves and corpuscles, flows and partial objects that are no longer dependent upon the large numbers; infinitesimal lines of escape, instead of the perspectives of the large aggregates" (280). —Gilles Deleuze and Félix Guattari, *Anti-Oedipus*

PIANO LOVE

I make love to a piano, jimmying my penis between the ivory of a sharp and a flat. I do not need to move forwards or backwards to make music. Rays assail my testicles and conjure my rich substance, which covers the earth but eludes the moon. Cursed, I return my penis to the angry shunt of my *vagina dentata*, focusing on the moment, deflecting the immanent certainty of mastication/castration. My unmanning will not be my undoing despite the clashing tectonics of its fury. This is the case even if my ability to picture my condition wanders into the tundra.

CROWDS AND POWER

On the back cover of *Crowds and Power*, an anthropological reevaluation of culture and society, Susan Sontag says that the author of the book, Elias Canetti, "dissolves politics and pathology, treating society as a mental activity—a barbaric one, of course—that must be decoded."

The blurb indicates what the text does without applauding it. At the same time, its existence as a blurb signifies applause. Ultimately, however, blurbs say and mean nothing. Like most written words, they are sheer consumer-capitalist feculence.

The first sentences of all texts say and mean everything. If the sentence fails to resonate, the text is worth nothing and should be set aside.

The first sentence of the first chapter of Schreber's *Memoirs*, for instance, reads: "The human soul is contained in the nerves of the body; about their physical nature I, as a layman, cannot say more than that they are extraordinarily delicate structures—comparable to the finest filaments—and that the total mental life of a human being rests on their excitability by external impressions" (19).

This does not red-flag a text that should be set aside. Nor does Canetti's first sentence: "There is nothing that man fears more than the touch of the unknown" (16).

A recipient of the Nobel Prize largely due to *Crowds and Power*, Canetti proceeds to explain how the formation, function and interplay of crowds are pathological symptoms of the desire and anxiety that characterize the human animal. He concludes with a long discussion of Schreber, using his delusion as a Ballardian extreme metaphor for civilization. Schreber "is left the sole survivor because this is what he himself wants. He wants to be the only man left alive, standing in an immense field of corpses; and he wants this field of corpses to contain all men but himself. It is not only as a paranoiac that he reveals himself here. To be the last man to remain alive is the deepest urge of every real seeker after power" (443).

Like Freud at the end of *Civilization and Its Discontents*, Canetti's final deduction strikes the same chord: mankind is an intelligent monster but a monster nonetheless. This is implied in his final sentence: "It is difficult to resist the suspicion that behind paranoia, as behind all power, lies the same profound urge: the desire to get other men out of the way so as to be the only one; or, in the milder, and indeed often admitted, form, to get others to help him *become* the only one" (462).

ROOM 003-1

"I am not the ghost of my former self."

She uses a low-grade fiction detector to scrutinize the manuscript as the scroll reads my vitals and pinpoints the last segment of the spacetime worm that describes my existence in the fourth dimension.

I don't know if the manuscript and the scroll are interchangeable parts, the same entity, or thoroughly different aliens.

BIBLIOGRAPHY [THE FATHER]

1909 marks the publication of the thirty-second edition of Moritz Schreber's bestselling book, *Medical Indoor Gymnastics, or, A System of Hygienic Exercises for Home Use to Be Practiced Anywhere Without Apparatus or Assistance by Young and Old of Either Sex, for the Preservation of Health and Global Activity.* Other popular works by Moritz include: *Physical Training from a Medical Standpoint, also a Matter of State; Detrimental Carriage and Habit of the Child; Callipaedics, or, Rearing unto Beauty Through the Natural and Uniform Promotion of Bodily Development; Anthropos: The Structural Wonder of the Human Organism; The Pangymnastikon, or, The Complete System of Gymnastics Using Only One Piece of Equipment;* and *The Family Friend as Educator and Conductor to Domestic Happiness, to Popular Health, and to the Refinement of Man for the Fathers and Mothers of the German People.*

ROOM 002-1

In slowtime, my fiberoptic semen exits the wound in my groin and fills the toilet basin as primal scenes timelapse across my screen of vision like fleeting-improvised clouds in the sky.

Ignoring the scroll of reality, my father pounds on the door and screams at me, promising to engorge and unbury me.

EXPERIMENTALISM

D. is shown a photograph of two men engaged in coitus. He shrugs.

D. is shown a video of a woman making love to her hand. He watches it blankly.

D. is jacked into the schizoverse via cortical shunt. He fucks and kills a transvestite, then is jacked out.

D. is stared at by a team of therapists, all of whom have trimmed their peppersalt beards into the same shape. He suspects they are wearing masks.

When you ask D. about his allergies, he ignores you. When you press him, urging him to tell you how he got those rashes, why he has diarrhea, why he wheezes like an elderly gorilla and his throat itches, he says: "Reality."

D. makes a mental note: "God is a double agent, but Freud is not Flechsig in disguise."

THE PATHOLOGICAL MACHINE [PART 2]

In *Dark City*, Proyas converts *Memoirs* into a story where *fantastical* facts manifest as *fictional* facts. Schreber's book presents the facts about his fantasies—which he believed to be factual. Proyas, in turn, appropriates certain aspects of Schreber's fantasies and actualizes them, translating subjective unreality into objective reality. But that objective reality operates in the diegesis of a filmic, fictional universe, and so the facts that Proyas (re) presents are not literally factual. Both texts operate under the aegis of the real while remaining equally grounded in the unreal and skirting the witch-hammer of signification.

SIGH-FI

Schreber's tentacles extend to the far reaches of the science fiction genre whether the genre knows it or not. The novels, stories, shifting realities and divine invasions of Philip K. Dick in particular are cut from the same cloth. PKD felt drawn to German culture and history and developed a familiarity with the language, as if Schreber might be calling out to him, or more accurately, haunting him. Consider all of the exegetical ghosts that flare up in his fiction—"little devils" and "fleeting-improvised men" scaling the walls of his psyche and running rampant through the transcendent interzones . . .

. . . in *A Scanner Darkly*. Narcs wear scramble suits to conceal their identities. The suit's design is described as "a multifaceted quartz lens hooked up to a miniaturized computer whose memory banks held up to a million and a half physiognomic fraction-representations of various people: men and women, children, with every variant encoded and then projected outward in all directions equally onto a superthin shroudlike membrane large enough to fit around an average human" (23). In *Memoirs*, Schreber "saw even articles of clothing on the bodies of human beings being transformed" (107) . . .

Dark City seems more like an adaptation of a PKD story than Schreber's *Memoirs*. And yet the spade of the Schreberian trumps the jack of the Phildickian. Aided by injections from Sutherland's mad Schreber-Scientist, the machinery of the spatial conurbation (a sprawl of noir high-rises encased in a containment field floating through outer space) mutates when the Strangers tune it. Thus, two mutations—one neuronic, the other architectural—continually retool the identities and subjectivities of the human lab rats whose clockwork they don't understand. The Strangers (dis)embody Schreber's mad God-Scientist, who experiments on him in order to unlock the hidden truth of his being, and the machinic city (dis)embodies the machinery of Schreber's mad Father-God-Scientist, who experimented on him as a boy . . .

What is at stake? What does it matter if PKD's science fiction reveals the same schizflows as Schreber's mechanized dreams? What does this intersection say about science fiction, which, in many ways, is no longer science fiction, but banal reality (i.e., sigh-fi)? The root of all origins is the spark of mad scientism, be it natural or supernatural, corporeal or cosmic. Neither subject, then, is terribly unique. And if sigh-fi is the Alpha and the Omega, the First and the Last, the Beginning and the End . . .

CIRCLE JERK

From Ubikuity: "Motion that is circular is the deadest form of the universe." —Philip K. Dick, A Scanner Darkly

There is a mad hooker outside my room.

ALIENISM

SCHIZE: According to the Interior Ministry, the route is a matter of discovery, i.e., ritual vanguards and images of éclairs have amounted to a conspiracy that will never escape the pole barn. The flesh giants have eaten the puppeteers in the rafters and there are no attack monkeys. "BONDAGE DIVAS HAND-CUFF GUARDS IN PRISON BREAK" (Armand 1). Blank screens are the new poetry under the viaducts of midnight. Ekphrasis. *Le cul du plombier.* Nobody rapes microphones in this two-dimensional universe. Above all, "plotlines belong in cemeteries" (ibid.).

THE SELF, THE I, THE NOT-ME RECOGNIZED AS "ME," ÜBERMENSCH, GOD, THE UNIVERSE, THE IMAGE WE SEE IN THE MIRROR AND PROJECT ONTO THE STAGE OF FOREVER

Insecurity is a matter of degrees and intensities that figures into the psychological fitness of all human beings, prompting them to action, reaction and/or inaction.

What we do (or don't do) is contingent upon an individual's measure of affect, which is itself continually (re)figured by the vicissitudes of social and neurological conditions.

If aliens dissected the human condition, they would note that Insecurity is among our definitive qualities. Without it, we would cease to be human.

Judgment begets Guilt and Shame, the wellsprings of Anxiety, which dictates the ebbs and flows of Insecurity.

To explore the topography of Insecurity, we must enter the courtroom and sequester the Judges.

There are multiple Judges, just as there are multiple Fathers, but the Fathers and the Judges are not necessarily the same Machine, and in the end, the only Judge and Father that matters is the Self, the I, the Not-Me recognized at "Me," Übermensch, God, the Universe, the Image we see in the mirror and project onto the stage of Forever—who everybody inevitably becomes.

A CONSPIRACY OF POSTURES

From the Book of Life: *"Books or other notes* are kept in which for years have been *written-down* all my thoughts, all my phrases, all my necessaries, all the articles in my possession or around me, all persons with whom I come into contact, etc. I cannot say with certainty who does the writing down. As I cannot imagine God's omnipotence lacks all intelligence, I presume that the writing-down is done by creatures given human shape on distant celestial bodies after the manner of fleeting-improvised men, but lacking all intelligence; their hands are led automatically, as it were, by passing rays for the purpose of making them write-down, so that later rays can again look at what has been written down" (123). —Daniel Paul Schreber, *Memoirs of My Nervous Illness*

This is not the Pipe.

ROOM 002-2

The hooker is my wife.

My hands open the door and she steps across the threshold.

ROOM 003-2

The hooker's tail hammers the bed like the trunk of a suffocating elephant as I take her from behind. Occasionally the tail strikes me in the head or chest and I fly across the room and slam into a wall. I always get back up and get back on her.

Her flesh is too cold to be alive.

Whenever my fingers try to grasp her hips, they slip off the scales and fall into the loam.

NIETZSCHE'S KISSES

In a novelization of the schizophrenic trauma that Friedrich Nietzsche experienced during his final night before succumbing to a mysterious mental condition (possibly induced by a syphilitic infection) that plagued him for the last decade of his life, Lance Olsen oscillates between different tenses, temporalities and settings to represents the nineteenth century German philosopher as a diseased human animal as much as an intellectual sage; in his head, he continues to philosophize with a hammer, but in reality, he pisses and shits down his leg like an infant, speculating about the meaning of the fecal act. Written in clear, crisp, dynamic prose, Olsen shows us the many faces of Nietzsche the Dionysian, the invalid, the lover, the asshole, the German, the brat, the poet, the whiner and the visionary. *Nietzsche's Kisses* is the Passion of the Anti-Christ.

Appropriately, the text of the novel is disjointed, fragmented, schized. Olsen often uses stream-of-consciousness to depict Nietzsche's voyage back and forth between the diegetic present and past, both of which are filtered through Nietzsche's complex subjectivity and emotional spectrum. The chapter parts and titles range from time periods ("5 p.m.," "6 p.m.," "7 p.m.," etc.) to body parts and internal organs ("tongue," "stomach," "teeth," "hands," "liver," "nervous system") to more philosophical tracks ("on the vision & the riddle," "raids of an untimely man," "on the spirit of gravity," "*historia abscondita*"). The first group charts the linear progression of time on Nietzsche's night of death. The third group refers to his writing ("on the vision & the riddle" and "on the spirit of gravity," among others, are chapter titles in *Thus Spoke Zarathustra*). The second group calls attention to one of the novel's dominant themes: *writing as organism*.

Repeatedly the human body (or bodily function) is connected to narrative and syntax: "*Every sentence is a kiss. . . . every paragraph* [is] *an embrace. . . .* They aren't sentences at all *sentences* being too soft a word for what they are they are *teeth. . . .* the corpse of philosophy . . . in the heart of a paragraph, you know your longitude and latitude" (15, 20, 44, 45, 149). This connection is most effectively conveyed in the following passage at the end of the chapter called "tongue": "writing isn't expansion but compression a texturing into fragment saying in seven sentences what everyone else says in a book saying in seven sentences what everyone else *doesn't* say in a book employing the figure or aphorism because you do not want to be read but learned by heart and this is how you will construct a particle philosophy for a particulate world bringing together what is shard and riddle and chance engineering with your flesh and from that day forward this will be what you will mean when you say the word *tongue*" (68).

Nietzsche wrote against this kind of subject matter throughout his career. Most nineteenth century Western philosophers viewed the body and the mind as two distinct parts of human nature constantly battling one another. Nietzsche rejected this dualism, arguing that the body and mind should be viewed as one entity, one self. The body is not a mere exterior inside of which the mind reigns supreme. Rather, it is an organism in which the mind functions on a subordinate level. The body is not the prison of the mind; the mind is the panopticon of the body.

Acknowledging and transcending this idea played a pivotal role in manifesting the body of the Übermensch. Nietzsche directly addresses non-believers in "On the Despisers of the Body," a chapter in *Thus Spoke Zarathustra*, claiming that they "are not bridges to the superman" and that the body is "a great intelligence, a multiplicity with one sense, a war and a peace, a herd and a herdsman" (61). Not coincidentally, part one of *Nietzsche's Kisses* is entitled "on the despisers of the body."

The great irony that Olsen's novel portrays is how Nietzsche's body became an enemy of his mind in his old age, if for no other reason than it prohibited him from writing and further pursuing his philosophical goals. The minutiae of reality and the tedium of the bodily apparatus become more difficult for Nietzsche to negotiate than the creation of a new ideology, culture and futurology. "Friedrich has smote history into two halves. Surely he can hold his fluids another few seconds" (51). Such passages elicit a sense of sympathy for Nietzsche contrary to most of his own narratives (including *Thus Spoke Zarathustra* as well as *Beyond Good & Evil*; *Twilight of the Idols*; *The Anti-Christ*; *Human, All Too Human*; and principally *Ecce Homo*) in which his speakers are invariably strong-willed, outspoken and often megalomaniacal. Olsen's Nietzsche is not Nietzsche's Nietzsche. And both figures are inevitable simulacra, one of Nietzsche as ordinary-genius-diseased-schizo, the other as utopian-romantic-*desideratum*-superhero.

ROOM 004-2

Over 900,000 words now. That's longer than most exegeses.

If years pass, so do minutes, but the passing of minutes does not necessarily amount to years.

There are 525,600 minutes in one year. Anything less is an exercise in nonsense.

In the absence of internal organs, my body hardly recognizes the symptoms of withdrawal, even if I continue to tremble like a leaf, and parts of my body have fallen asleep and gone numb, like mankind.

THE MASTER BITCH

"What is on your mouth?" asks **Y**.

"My mouth?" **X** touches his mouth. "Nothing. It's my mouth. My mouth is on my mouth. Right?"

"I see."

"**X** marks the spot." **X** touches his mouth.

"That's not funny."

"I know. I'm a serious person. Like my poems."

Y sighs. "Yes. Your poems."

"Don't worry," **X** assures him. "The feminine nature of poetry speaks to my own evolving femininity. This is the nature of art in general. It's a woman's business, you know."

"Is that right?"

"That's right."

"Interesting."

X sucks in his cheeks. "My head is a theater of word hordes that collide and explode like mad symphonies. The theater is too vast and complex to represent in its totality. I can only show you bits and pieces. These are my poems."

Y furrows his brown, then blinks. "I was wrong. There's nothing on your mouth."

"I prefer haiku, but I am perfectly capable of writing sonnets, ballads, limericks, elegies and rap songs. Fuck epic poetry! Fuck it! I can say more in a haiku than an epic poem."

"You have dry lips, is all. I can't tolerate dry lips. I don't understand them." **Y** shifts uncomfortably in his seat. "If one has dry lips, one licks one's lips and moistens them. In extreme circumstances, one applies lip balm. What one doesn't do is leave the lips to themselves."

X touches his mouth.

Y flexes his jaw.

"Soon I will vent enough poems and transform myself into a master poet," says **X**. "This will coincide with the swelling of my breasts and the emergence of my cunt, a vagina dentata that will eat my cock and deliver the wreckage to my anus. The hair on my skin is already falling off. Look." He bares his forearms. "As I utter my final couplet and become what I am destined to be, God will bend me over and make me a master bitch, fucking me at last. God knows nothing of poetry. God is a mechanic. God is a plumber. And I am a toilet clogged with—"

"Melodrama. Subterfuge. Another attempt to deflect the compulsion to masturbate."

"Finally God will impregnate me. In so doing, he will empty me. And then I will give birth to Myself."

"Anti-masturbatory rhetoric," snorts **Y**. "No matter how hard you try, you will never escape the grin of the Phallus."

X touches his mouth.

"MISS"

One of the only English words to appear in *Memoirs*.

ÉCRITURE DE MERDE

Michel de Certeau makes a vital point in "The Institution of Rot": "A piece of graffiti in a movie theater in Paris offered readers a transgression rejected by the institution: 'Don't write in the shitters, shit on writing.' Schreber went from one of these deviancies to the other" (98).

THE STRIPPER AND THE SCHIZO

Between the aural interstices of 10,000 children screaming and splashing in an indoor pool, the schizo hears too much of the Real, a shapeshifter that constantly does a striptease before him, peeling off her skin and organs, but she never succeeds in fully denuding herself. Hence the schizophrenic must become the stripper. In effect, he can show herself their bones.

SKULL

The puzzle pieces
break off like sun-dried lobster
and I bleed syntax.

CHRONOLOGY

1842   Daniel Paul Schreber is born for the first time.

1843   Daniel Paul Schreber speaks for the first time.

1844   Daniel Paul Schreber defecates in a toilet for the first time.

1846   Daniel Paul Schreber is spanked for the first time.

1847   Daniel Paul Schreber is experimented on by his father for the first time.

1848   Daniel Paul Schreber stares at the sun for the first time.

1854   Daniel Paul Schreber is bullied for the first time.

1855   Daniel Paul Schreber tortures insects for the first time.

1857   Daniel Paul Schreber looks at pornography for the first time.

1860   Daniel Paul Schreber smokes a pipe for the first time.

1861   Daniel Paul Schreber solicits a prostitute for the first time.

1871   Daniel Paul Schreber is abducted by "Strangers" for the first time.

1884   Daniel Paul Schreber dies for the first time.

1885   Daniel Paul Schreber is reborn for the first time.

1886   Daniel Paul Schreber witnesses murder for the first time.

1893   Daniel Paul Schreber molests his own soul for the first time.

1894   Daniel Paul Schreber wears a straightjacket for the first time.

1895   Daniel Paul Schreber witnesses an apocalypse for the first time.

1896   Daniel Paul Schreber uses a tampon for the first time.

1897   Daniel Paul Schreber enters and inhabits the Lacanian Real for the first time.

1898   Daniel Paul Schreber eats his own body for the first time.

1900   Daniel Paul Schreber becomes God for the first time.

1911   Daniel Paul Schreber dies for the last time.

I stopped consuming liquids long ago. Solid food remains a necessity. I clean the plates of whatever is left for me.

My syntax is more feces than fertility. The disease of meaning has infested my core.

I wear my nerves on my skin. Contrary to popular belief, the nerves do not look like veins. They are beautiful, almost sublime, with a radiant, ladylike quality that attracts my gaze whenever I pass by the mirrors.

Nobody has pounded on the door or screamed at me for centuries.

Drooling in silence, the scroll looms over me like a saltwater crocodile standing on its hind legs.

ROOM 006-2

Not a crocodile. A prehistoric bird. It has four wings. The scales and enormity of the current status of the scroll dictated my hasty first impression.

"I lived for years in doubt as to whether I was really still on earth or whether on some other celestial body," says the bird. "Even in the year 1895 I still considered the possibility of my being on Phobos, a satellite of the planet Mars which had once been mentioned by the voices in some other context, and wondered whether the moon, which I sometimes saw in the sky, was not the main planet Mars" (Schreber 81).

Speaking in a British accent with German undertones, the fanged beak is soft and pliable and sculpts the words like long Augustinian lips.

"I am not the germ of my future doppelgänger," I say, spinning my identity.

Finally the Director breaks the Fourth Wall. He doesn't like my dialogue. He doesn't like my acting. He doesn't like me. Reshoot. The mise-en-scène stays as it lays.

The next and last time I see the Director is in a hypnogogic dream.

BLICKSPRACHE [TRANS. GAZE LANGUAGE]

The Devil's Castle eluded Schreber's ability to describe it in operable languages. The architecture, the spatial arrangement, even the bricks and the mortar—they belonged to another dimension. He could only describe it in an extra-dimensional, non-transvariable language rooted not in rhetoric but in flicks of the eye, transcendentally articulate nuances of the gaze communicated with birdlike acuity. The question lingers as to who was his audience, i.e., his interlocutor or "reader," but this didn't concern him. He was vehemently opposed to the general idea of the reader, who did little but inhibit the prowess and innovation of the Author. In a perfect world, he would kill the reader and ensure the birthright of his primacy. Whatever the case, one day the reader will be dead to the Author. Then, finally, the Author can begin to think about freedom.

DIVINE EROTOMANIA

Y: "The sun is a whore" (Schreber 331).

X: "What?"

Y: "Turn to page 331."

X blinks at Y, then bows his head and fumbles through the book. "Oh," he says.

Y: "Read that passage aloud."

X: "You read it. I wrote it."

Y: "I'm sorry. That's not how the Order of the World works."

X glares at Y, then bows his head and fumbles through the book. "The more the signifier signifies nothing, the more indestructible it is—" (Lacan, *The Psychoses* 185).

Y: "That passage isn't in that book. You didn't write it. Page 331. The underlined passage."

X: "Don't tell me what I didn't write. I know which page is the wrong page."

Y: "Do you?"

X fumbles through the book. *"The sun is a whore . . .* This passage is underlined in green ink. Moreover, it has been underlined with a ruler. Who underlines texts with a ruler?"

Y: "Is that the question you want to ask? Is that the sum total of your traumatic kernels—a straight line?"

X throws the book at a wall. "Without straight lines, there is no geometry. Without geometry, there is no Order of the World. Without the Order of the World, there is no God, because the Order of the World did not create itself. A house can't build itself. Nor can a universe. Whether you believe an afterlife or not doesn't matter. The objective existence of an afterlife matters even less. I'm talking about creation. Primordial sparks. *Straight lines.* And the whore who draws them, intersects them, triangulates them. There can only be a supernatural explanation."

Y: "God underlined that passage, then?"

X: "God and the sun are interchangeable parts. Everything, technically, is an interchangeable part, locking and unlocking into place."

Y: "That doesn't answer my question."

Eyeballing **Y**, **X** tears a hangnail from an index finger with his teeth. He chews it, swallows it. "<u>Go fuck yourself</u>. Therein lies eternity."

CALL AND RESPONSE

From the Cubicle: "You asked me recently why I maintain that I am afraid of you. As usual, I was unable to think of any answer to your question, partly for the very reason that I am afraid of you, and partly because an explanation of the grounds for this fear would mean going into far more details than I could even approximately keep in mind while talking. And if I now try to give you an answer in writing, it will still be very incomplete, because, even in writing, this fear and its consequences hamper me in relation to you and because the magnitude of the subject goes far beyond the scope of my memory and power of reasoning" (116). —Franz Kafka, "Letter to His Father"

SCHIZE: "We will be approaching Schreber's universe as if it were the obverse of Kafka's. It is a world equally exposed to something rotten in law, but that exposure takes place from the opposite side—from the side of the judge rather than that of the supplicant to the law" (Santner 13).

FOOTNOTE: Kafka's "Letter to His Father" could just as easily be Schreber writing to Moritz-Machine-Flechsig-God-Language-Self.

SWEET TRANSVESTITE

Like many transvestites, Schreber was afflicted by a profound internal Lack. He wanted to fill the Lack—that way, he would become healthy and whole. Citing *Memoirs*, Hunter and MacAlpine explain: "Schreber was now a transvestite: he 'moves about his room half naked, stands in front of the mirror in a very low-cut vest, decorated with gay ribbons, gazing at what he believes his female bosom.' He 'liked to occupy himself by looking at pictures of naked women, even drew them, and had his moustache removed.' He believed that his body was covered in female nerves . . . He bought sewing material and female toilet articles and took 'pleasure . . . in small feminine occupations, for instance sewing, dusting, making beds, washing up, and so on.' The 'cultivation of femaleness' became essential for his well-being'" (404).

Freud mistook Schreber's desire to unman himself for a desire to be gay. Or act gay. Or be himself. In fact, his transvestitism calls attention to the very phallogocentrism and compulsory heterosexuality that Judith Butler says are the genealogical effects of the history of power as exerted and facilitated by the male gaze. "Better to become a woman than to fuck a man," whispered Schreber's unconscious, a commonplace byproduct of his social and cultural matrix. But he had no more desire for same-sex relations than what is common among straight men (i.e., infrequent homosexual dreams). Moreover, he was trying less to seek agency from unwanted masculinity than from uninvited divinity, and becoming a woman was the only viable solution he could concoct as the flames of paranoia rose and fell, rose and fell from the embers of psychosis.

TEETH

These deposits of
calcium are symptoms of
my blood-soaked pubis.

I, BECOMING-WOMAN

One unexplored interpretation of Schreber's delusion about being transformed into a woman concerns his inability to father a child with his wife. They adopted a daughter because one of them was infertile. It didn't matter which one—in both cases, the failure belonged to Schreber, who was either shooting blanks or selected a barren spouse. Schreber the becoming-woman can be read as an indicator of his desire to father the child that would remake himself, rendering the child a new and improved version of the prodigal father. Only supernatural forces could put his plan into motion, i.e., only a classically enacted deus ex machina could set the record straight. God's intervention would lend Schreber the scepter of control. God is a man and has a penis. In order to harness God's power/phallus, Schreber needed to become a woman so that God could impregnate him, at which point he would grow and give (re)birth to himself. Then, as a demigod (à la the angels of Milton's *Paradise Lost*), he would be in a position to usurp God and steal all of the milk from the udders of His powertrain. Allowing himself to become a woman and get fucked, in other words, was a trick, and he was a Shakespearean clown, smarter and craftier than the royalty he pretended to entertain.

ORIGINAL SKETCH AND NOTE-TO-SELF FOR *FLECHSIG: A FLEETING-IMPROVISED NOVEL*

Keep it short and don't fuck with capable readers (assuming they exist). Each chapter should be a prose poem, etc. If you extract old criticism, do it piecemeal. PLOT: Schreber rises to power as a would-be messiah and commandeers the authority of father-Flechsig, who becomes his minion and disciple. Develop three antagonists, one of which is Flechsig's assistant, Dr. Täuscher. Thread the superzero but don't fully inhabit it. REMEMBER: Science fiction is a ghost; the New is not in the Next or in the Now but in the *Never*.

ROOM 007-2

"It is neither my intention nor my pleasure to give birth to a master race," I tell a hooker matter-of-factly. "I am not doing this. This is being done to me."

Making a face, I technologize her.

I am trying to impregnate everybody now.

My dealer takes me aside to reprimand me. I technologize her.

Somebody accuses me of "fungus rape." I have never seen my accuser before. Everybody, in fact, has become a Stranger.

Even the bed, the end tables, the light fixtures, the wallpaper, the drapes, the carpet, the Victrola . . . none of it looks familiar.

The identity of the scroll stays intact.

THE PATHOLOGICAL MACHINE [PART 3]

Superior and subjugated in chorus, Schreber is as much a god as he is a slave, even if the latter polarity dominates his experience.

The image of Schreber as a clockwork mechanism, as a machine that is continually programmed and reprogrammed by external and internal forces, pervades *Memoirs* and is the most visible feature appropriated by Alex Proyas in *Dark City*.

The Strangers' reconstruct the urban landscape from their subterranean liar, which is fittingly distinguished by a gigantic illuminated clock indicating when it is time for the city to be "tuned," a process that demands collective and cathectic energy to shut down the city and rewire city-goers. Tuning is "the ultimate technology, the ability to alter physical reality by will alone." Dressed in tight black outfits reminiscent of SS uniforms, the Strangers recall Clive Barker's extra-dimensional cenobites with their deathly pale skin and bald heads as they psychically reconfigure the architecture of the city through the medium of the underground machine, which allows them to amplify their thoughts.

Schreber's mechanized body has been effectively translated to the body of the metropolis in *Dark City*. Proyas has literalized and, as it were, *metropolized* the judge's machinic self. His city is a robotic Frankenstein monster that looms over and antagonizes the human subjects it accommodates; at the same time, it is subject to the behind-the-scenes clockwork that empowers it. Schreber is all of these things in *Memoirs*: master and slave, protagonist and antagonist, engine and apparatus. He is a superhero/super-zero who assails himself with the technology of his pathology.

BIRDS OF A FEATHER

For the final attack scene in the upstairs bedroom, Hitchcock hooked bird puppets, bird corpses and live birds to Tippi Hedren's dress with rubber bands. Rolling the camera, he flung half-strangled birds at her from a closet as crewmen dumped nests into the room from a hole in the ceiling. Whenever Hedren screamed that enough was enough, Hitchcock screamed louder and flung birds harder, insisting that enough was never enough. It was only when she passed out that he cut the action. Then he woke her with smelling salts and a Neurobion injection for another take.

For Schreber, birds are nerves in disguise, putting him in "a mysterious connection with the innermost nature of divine creation" (Schreber 190). Furthermore, the fact that *the nerves which are inside these birds are remnants* (single nerves) *of souls of human beings who had become blessed* is absolutely certain because of [his] observations repeated thousands of times every day for years" (ibid).

In English, the onomatopoeic sound of a signing bird is *chirp chirp* or *tweet tweet*. In German, it is *piep piep* or *tschiep*.

BIRDS OF A FATHER

Schreber only cites his father by name once in reference to Moritz's *Manual of Bedroom Gymnastics*, wondering if what the voices tell him about mainstream lovemaking positions between men and women are true. Hence Lacan: "The prevalence, in the entire evolution of Schreber's psychosis, of paternal characters who replace one another, grow larger and larger and envelope one another to the point of becoming identified with the divine Father himself, a divinity marked by the properly paternal accent, is undeniable, unshakable" (*The Psychoses* 315).

FATHER SUN

From the Continuity Shot: "In Schreber's case, the focus on the source of endless energy supplies filling the lack up to the limit of what can be held in reserve on earth proposes the ultimate union, which is not interpersonally conjugated, say, between man and woman, but intrapsychically and extraterrestrially constituted between Mother Earth and Father Sun. Nuclear fusion on earth is the psychotic or science fiction alternative that breaks out of what's going down in the immediate family" (147). —Laurence A. Rickels, *Nazi Psychoanalysis: Psy-Fi*

RAP SONG [CHORUS]

God is a pimp and I am his ho.
See me turnin' tricks as I work the dance flo.
God sez yo bitch gimme some ass.
I sez yo God no need to be crass.
This is your world
And I am your girl
Till I turn the turntable,
Till I make you my fable.

Then you be my ho
And I pimp yo mojo
And we take this shit to the thousandth plateau.

ROOM 008-2

My children remind me of my afterimage as much as my primordial soup.

One of them is slipping into futurity even as the quicksand of history yanks him into the earth.

There is a swath of red rust on his leg.

His skin cracks before my eyes like old, white leather.

The drool spilling from the spigot of his lower lip is thick and gray and smells like sewage.

In order to simulate affection, I touch him . . . and a loud, tall flame swallows my fingertip.

Red irises. No pupils.

I need another fix.

THE PATHOLOGICAL MACHINE [PART 4]

Dark City extrapolates numerous other features in *Memoirs*. As I indicated earlier, for instance, the Strangers are small, scorpionlike creatures that occupy the skull cavities of human corpses and act as the corpses' brains—a blatant allusion to Schreber's belief that there were "scorpions" living in his head. There is also Schreber's recurrent feeling that he walked among corpses. This is quite true in the film, as John Murdoch lives in a city infested by the dead bodies that the Strangers use as vessels. Additional extrapolations include the following:

SOUL MURDER. *Memoirs*: "The idea is widespread in the folklore and poetry of all peoples that it is somehow possible to take possession of another person's soul in order to prolong one's life at another soul's expense" (33). *Dark City*: On the brink of extinction, the Strangers want to take possession of Murdoch's soul in order to prolong and vitalize their race.

TERMINAL NIGHT. *Memoirs*: Schreber maintained that single nights often seemed to last for hundreds of years. *Dark City*: There is no day. It is always nighttime.

DIVINE RAYS. *Memoirs*: God attempted to change Schreber's will and body by beaming rays at him. "My nerves have been set in motion *from without* incessantly and without any respite. Divine rays above all have the power of influencing the nerves of a human being" (55). *Dark City*: The Strangers change the architecture of the city by beaming rays at the tuning machine. Rays also allow them to move animate and inanimate objects.

PICTURING. *Memoirs*: "By vivid imagination I can produce pictures of all recollections from my life, of persons, animals and plants, of all sorts of objects in nature and objects of daily use, so that these images become visible either inside my head or if I wish, outside, where I want them to be seen by my own nerves and by the rays. I can do the same with weather phenomenon and other events; I can for example let it rain or let lightning strike—this is a particularly effective form of 'picturing'" (210). *Dark City*: The city is a manifestation of the recollections of "stolen [human] memories, different eras, different pasts all rolled into one." Furthermore, Murdoch develops the capacity to reproduce the physical environment. At the end of the film, he makes a sun, beach and ocean.

MEMORY EXTERMINATION. *Memoirs*: "The inner table of my skull was lined with a different brain membrane in order to extinguish my memory of my own ego" (97). *Dark City*: The Strangers continually extinguish the memories of humans and replace them with new ones, analyzing how they will react to and function in different socioeconomic contexts.

JESUS CHRIST. *Memoirs*: Schreber equates his sufferings with Christ's martyrdom. *Dark City*: Murdoch is a Christlike figure. In a culminating scene, he is even bound to the tuning apparatus with arms splayed out. And the image on the film jacket shows him crucified against the tuning machine's clock face.

Proyas capitalizes on *Memoirs* most explicitly by turning Schreber into an actual character: Murdoch's psychiatrist. This is an ironic twist if we consider it in light of the book, the nemesis of which is Schreber's god-psychiatrist, Dr. Flechsig. *Dark City's* Dr. Schreber is a jaded, nervy eccentric who assists the Strangers in their routine experiments on humans. For the first part of the film, we are led to believe he is allied with the Strangers by choice. We come to learn he has been forced to work for them and his intentions towards Murdoch are good-willed. He concocts a serum that provides Murdoch with a lifetime of rigorous instruction during which his supernatural powers are fully cultivated and ready to be used against his oppressors. Dr. Schreber enables Murdoch to actualize his innate godliness, overthrow the Strangers, and recreate the world in his own image. In his case study, Freud explains that the Schreber of *Memoirs* unconsciously replaces Flechsig with God (123). God is both patron and persecutor, and eventually Schreber projects this image onto himself. He becomes the ultimate tuner in his diegetic universe, and like an author, he renders the other characters in his story mere fictions that he can revise at will—the core energic desire of all human beings.

ALL NONSENSE CANCELS ITSELF OUT

X: "Am I **X** or **Y**?"

Y: "Who do you want to be?"

X: "I want to be me. Which one is that?"

Y: "That's up to you."

X: "Nothing is up to me. I'm fucking insane."

Y: "Insanity is a matter of perception."

X: "My perception is that I'm fucking insane. That's your perception, too."

Y: "My perception is irrelevant."

Beat.

X: "Am I X or Y?"

Y: "I don't know who you are."

X: "What's my family paying you for then?"

Y: "To keep you warm. To stop you from harming yourself."

X: "You're the one that's trying to kill me, fucker."

Y: "I have never tried to kill you."

X laughs like the Joker.

Y: "I have no reason to lie to you."

X: "You told me I wasn't God yesterday. Explain yourself."

Y: "Sometimes your eloquence subverts your nonsense."

Beat.

X: "All nonsense cancels itself out."

EYES

I have no control
when I ogle my breasts. My
eyes are not my own.

SCHREBERN

v. Synonym for gardening. *derv.* Dr. Daniel Gottlieb Moritz Schreber's theories on and practices of physical activities in fresh air. *ref. Schrebergarten* (trans. Schreber's garden).

MEIN KAMPF: A ONE-ACT PLAY

DRAMATIS PERSONAE

Daniel
The Director

Enter DANIEL. Gnarled and twitching, he staggers to the apron of the stage. Occasionally he pauses and bellows like an aggrieved dog. Once he reaches his mark, he stops twitching, straightens himself out, tilts up his chin and delivers a powerful crowdstare, standing there like a dictator about to address his people.

DANIEL [*to the audience*]: I will fuck you! I will fuck you! I will—!

THE DIRECTOR [*offstage*]: Cut! [*Steps onstage.*] You can't swear, Dan. That's not even the line. Let's start from the top. [*To the audience.*] Sorry, folks.

DANIEL *looks back and forth between the audience and* THE DIRECTOR, *deciding what to do, then slumps his shoulders and lopes offstage. He never returns.*

ROOM 009-2

Everybody's aura pixilates and floats into the sky one proton at a time. All of the electrons have died on the vine. Neutrons, like quarks, are a myth. Nihility is the solar reality.

My dealer tells me that, while emotions live in the organs, the aura concerns God. "The aura is God's domain," she says, fixing me.

I technologize eternity. "I still feel like shit," I confess.

"Feeling badly is the stinking fertilizer of being alive," says a melting, skewered mouth. "Nothing gets done in the absence of negative energy."

I negate the mouth and appropriate the worm.

Humming like an orchestra of monks, the sun evaporates all of the oceans and lakes and tarns and scorches the green wilderness. The razorsharp sand crystals that comprise the residual desert cut into my swollen segments as I inch forward; I can hear my blood singe in the heat, and within seconds, all of my organs have burst aflame.

As I vomit lava into the toilet and burn up the water, the porcelain and the pipes, I hear my father speaking to me with the heavy breath of a divine minion: "I have no doubt that God, in His relation to me, is ruled by egoism. This might be calculated to confuse religious feelings as God Himself would then not be the ideal Being of absolute love and morality, as most religions imagine. *Egoism is a necessary quality of all living beings*; individuals cannot do without it, if they are not themselves to perish; in itself it therefore does not appear reprehensible" (Schreber 307). This is the first of several monologues that conclude with a pat assertion: "Only I, and no other human being, have the right to mock God" (289).

I pass out.

When I awake, I discover that I have molted my skin and eaten part of the scroll.

DOCTRINES OF SALVATION

The Phildickian transmogrification into a "woman" is endowed with soteriological significance/signification. Only Mother Nature can consum(mat)e Father Culture, eating from the inside-out that which was constructed by Machinic Desire from the outside-in. As Doctor Moreau's Beast Folk chant: "None escape" (Wells 62).

ONANISM

SIDEBAR: "Von W. was the man who was supposed to have accused Schreber of onanism. The 'little men' are described by Schreber himself as being among the most remarkable and, in some respects, the most puzzling phenomena of his illness. It looks as though they were the product of a condensation of children and—spermatozoa" (Freud, "Psychoanalytic Notes" 132).

THE OTHERS

There are moments where I'm not afraid of anything or anyone. There are moments where I fear everything and everyone. Some moments are unbearable, but I always know that a bearable moment will supplant it. Periodically I experience moments of concerted apathy that border on contentment. They are worth their wait in *différance*.

[WO]MAN

Niederland summarizes Schreber's delusional system as follows: "He felt he had a mission to redeem the world and to restore it to its lost state of bliss. This mission must be preceded by the destruction of the world and by personal transformation into a woman. Transformed into a female, he—Schreber, now a woman—would become God's mate, and out of such union a better and healthier race of men would emerge" (10).

SCHIZE: In order to become a (better) man, Schreber needed to become a (breeding) woman.

NICHT SCHREBER

REMEMBER: This is not a book about Daniel Paul Schreber. Nor is it translatable in the absence of gravid counterparts and specular images. Readers will not assimilate this book by way of identification—the laws of enormity and obscurantism prohibit it.

At best, this book is a gateway drug; at worst, a harmless turd.

LOONEY TUNE

God does not understand human beings, but in his dreams, He wants to find a way to relate to us (to our *modes de vie*, to our social and sexual kinks, to our need for taboos and ennui and violence, etc.).

He appreciates silent prayers more than spoken words. All human voices sound the same and assail His eardrums like kamikaze insects. Neither method brings him closer to enlightenment.

The only thing about human behavior that God can begin to wrap His head around is music. Especially rap, jazz and Beethoven.

Citing *Memoirs*, Rosemary Dinnage writes: "God, like the paterfamilias of the childcare manuals, '*did not really understand the living human being* and had no need to understand him, because, according to the Order of the World, He dealt only with corpses'; this has 'run like a red thread through my entire life'" (xvi).

Despite the vicissitudes of Schreber's ideas about God's desires and acculturation, however, God often thinks about non-corpses, if only because of their altogether "otherworldly" nature. In His view, earth is a UFO and human beings are an alien race.

SCHIZE: Schreber is Captain Kirk as much as he is Marvin the Martian.

SECRETARIES TO THE INSANE

From the New Underworld: "We are apparently willingly going to become secretaries to the insane. This expression is generally used to reproach alienists for their impotence. Well then, not only shall we be his secretaries, but we shall take what he recounts literally—which till now has always been considered as the thing to avoid doing" (206). —Jacques Lacan, *The Psychoses*

NORMATIVE SINGULARITIES

Diseases of the mind are normative singularities.

Derived from the Greek, *neurosis* originally meant "nerve, tendon or sinew, structures which were not differentiated" whereas it was believed that *psychosis*, introduced much later, in 1845, constituted not an illness of the brain but of the mind and soul (Hunter and MacAlpine 16).

Perceptions changed, accelerating via Freud, producing new and different readings and treatments of the singularities.

During Schreber's life, the treatment involved confinement to an asylum.

In 1955, he "would certainly have qualified for electroshock, insulin hypoglycemia and leucotomy. One wonders what would have happened to the author of the Memoirs had his brain been submitted to such procedures. It is certain that the Memoirs could not have been written; whether he would have recovered as much as he did spontaneously is doubtful" (18).

In the twenty-first century, Schreber may have blended into society like the axiomatic teardrop in rain, finding a career as an alcoholic, chainsmoking screenwriter or website designer while minimizing bouts of psychosis, depression and anxiety with prescriptions of Risperdal, Zoloft and Klonopin.

ROOM θ1θ-1

I adjust the antennae again, extending one ear and bending another. Finally the picture clears.

There is a news story.

A reporter wearing red lipstick and a white blazer narrates her death by car crash. "The vehicle is coming at me," she announces into a microphone, facing the audience but peering off-camera. "I will be dead in seconds." She clears her throat. "I can see the people driving the vehicle. I can describe them. They are angry. They are vicious. They are free." She screams and pinches shut her eyes. The action slips into slow motion as the grill of a black truck strikes her and her body shatters like porcelain, dousing the screen with blood and bone and brains and flesh. After the truck rumbles away, a voice speaks from behind the gore. "I am dead now," it rattles. "I told you this would happen. Don't worry. Nobody is special. Everybody is replaceable. There are no exceptions."

It's true. When a hooker dies, 200,000 voluptuous souls rise from her grave. Overwhelmed by the exponential trauma, the pimps commit mass suicide and ascend into the Forecourts of Heaven.

The room extends into the distance for miles. Furniture and fixtures and technologies from different time periods expand and contract, collapse into nothingness and burst into being, shapeshifting, endlessly reconfiguring themselves around the host of Strangers that populate the red-rimmed expanse and move about in a timelapse of panic and purpose.

Interrupting the schizflow, I order a Stranger to crucify herself against the wall. She is apprehensive at first, but quickly acquiesces. Everybody and everything listens to me now.

I tell her I was kidding about the crucifixion. Her breasts fall off.

"Those were stickers."

I take her in my arms and kiss her deeply. I can taste the oil in her long throat. I can smell her rank breath through her loud nostrils. Her skin comes off in my hands as I caress her back and buttocks, but I keep going, kissing her harder, slipping fingers into her holes and massaging her genitals, which come apart . . . and then I am on the carpet as if poured there, a muddy lump, wet and heavy and flat.

Dissatisfied, I eat the rest of the scroll.

POSTHUMOUS [ANTI]OEDIPALIZATION

From the Machine: "On several occasions Freud's text marks the extent to which he felt the difficulty: to begin with, it appears difficult to assign as a cause of the malady—even if only an occasional cause—an 'outburst of homosexual libido' directed at Dr. Flechsig's person. But when we replace the doctor with the father and commission the father to explain the God of delirium, we ourselves have trouble following this ascension; we take liberties that can be justified only by the advantages they afford us in our attempt to understand the delirium. Yet the more Freud states such scruples, the more he thrusts them aside and sweeps them away with a firm and confident repose. And this response is double: it is not my fault if psychoanalysis attests to a great monotony and encounters the father everywhere—in Flechsig, in the God, in the sun; it is the fault of sexuality and its stubborn symbolism. Furthermore, it is not surprising that the father returns constantly in current deliriums in the most hidden and least recognizable guises, since he returns in fact everywhere and more visibly in religions and ancient myths, which express forces of mechanisms eternally active in the unconscious. It should be noted that Judge Schreber's destiny was not merely that of being sodomized, while still alive, by the rays from heaven, but also that of being posthumously oedipalized by Freud. From the enormous political, social, and historical content of Schreber's delirium, *not one word is retained*, as though the libido did not bother itself with such things. Freud invokes only a sexual argument, which consists in bringing about the union of sexuality and the familial complex, and a mythological argument, which consists in positing the adequation of the productive force of the unconscious and the 'edifying forces of myths and religions'" (57). —Gilles Deleuze and Félix Guattari, *Anti-Oedipus*

THE FRANKENSTEIN BARRIER

No matter what direction we move in or how many steps we take, we always-already find ourselves stumbling across the Arctic Circle holding hands with the yellow-eyed daemon. Mad scientism as conventional, i.e., contradistinguished and negated.

PREFASCIST PARANOIA OF THE POSTFASCIST VARIETY

And *Memoirs* as a kind of Nazi bible, as a precursor to "that more famous paranoid autobiography composed in confinement, Hitler's *Mein Kampf*" (Santner ix). Apropos: "Gradually I became uncertain" (Hitler 59).

FIXATION, AFTER-EXPULSION, IRRUPTION

Three phases of REPRESSION: FIXATION, AFTER-EXPUL-
SION ("repression proper"), IRRUPTION ("*return of the
repressed*") (Freud, "Psychoanalytic Notes" 143-44).

INTESTINES

A spacetime worm that
begins with a bang and ends
with a crunch. Ibid.

SEMINAL CORD

The pornographic
cosmos. The inguinal ring.
The junk of legend.

ILL COMMUNICATION

"The sun is not God's eye."

"How does God see?"

"My asshole is God's eye. It is always open. God is a cyclops and has insomnia."

"This is not a nightclub. You are not a standup comedian."

"God is a weak, insecure deity."

"He must be a Roman."

"You goddamn pimp."

"That's not funny. Nothing you say is funny."

"What's the point in speaking?"

"The presentation and exchange of information."

"Idle communication."

"Yes."

"What about expressing emotion? What about *ill* communication?"

"For effect only. One doesn't have to speak to be emotional."

"What about asking for directions?"

"If you don't know where you are, you shouldn't be going anywhere."

"What about fuckwords?"

"Fuckwords?"

"You know, dirty talk. Fuckwords."

"That's not funny."

"Which part? The signifier? The signified? Or the referent? There is no referent."

"That's not funny either."

"No. Nothing anybody says is funny."

"Yes."

"One must always be serious. There is no room for unseriousness. To be unserious—that would be wrong."

"It's not a moral issue. It's a matter of fact. *Fin.*"

"*Ende.*"

"Right."

"Ha ha."

THE PATHOLOGICAL MACHINE [PART 5]

By (re)making Dr. Schreber (via Kiefer Sutherland) into the narrator and primary source of exposition, Proyas destabilizes the diegesis of *Dark City*. We are to some degree constrained to view the film through the filter of his subjectivity. To what extent is the story being exploited by the director? Can we assume that what we are seeing is actually taking place? Or are we witnessing the fantasies of a psychotic, as we do when we read the real Schreber's book? Perhaps the Strangers and their experimental world are symptoms of the doctor's paranoid schizophrenia. The film might be a wish-fulfillment fantasy in which John Murdoch is an idealized version of Dr. Schreber, who lacks the power and stamina to overcome the Strangers himself. There's no way to tell. The action and events presented in *Dark City* are chronically subject to a pregnant hermeneutic of suspicion.

CHRONOLOGY

1967   Resurrected as an extra in the "Dawn of Man" sequence of *2001: A Space Odyssey* (1968), supplanting the consciousness of a mime in an ape suit. Confused, gesticulates and bellows uncontrollably, which is precisely what Kubrick wants. Escapes Shepperton Studios and gets lost in the London Tube, where commuters, perceiving him as a homeless man, either beat him or give him money. Tries repeatedly to get out of ape suit but there are no zippers; he's sewed in. Evaporates, taking the mime with him, and leaving the thin, capable body to rot beneath a WAY OUT sign.

I am climbing down the rungs for the last time. The scroll is gone. I am the scroll. My skin and organs have fallen off. My skeleton melted off. I am a simple geometry now, a sequence of straight lines and common denominators capped by teeth, tongue, eyeballs and a brain.

Epiphanies drip from my integers and fall into the Abyss, never to be seen or heard, tasted or touched, cultivated or cremated by anyone but me.

One of the epiphanies says: "Optimism is not a choice; it's a way of losing."

Another one says: "All dark matter violates its essence."

Another one says: "On the outside, I am a monster is a pulp science fiction *novel*. On the inside, I am a monster in a pulp science fiction *movie*."

Every bead of knowledge escapes me before I can digest it.

As I pick up speed, a thousand voices explode into the echo chamber. They fuse into one, fully calibrated Voice that pretends to be me but is probably the Devil, or God, or a Stranger, or my dealer, or nobody . . .

"When I am melting I have no hands," intones the Voice. "I go into a doorway in order not to be trampled on. Everything is flying away from me. In the doorway I can gather the pieces of my body. It is as if something is thrown in me, bursts me asunder. Why do I divide myself in different pieces? I feel that I am without poise, that my personality is melting and that my ego disappears and that I do not exist anymore. Everything pulls me apart. The skin is the only possible means of keeping the different pieces together. There is no connection between the different parts of my body" (Sass, *Madness* 15).

Per usual, I am denied the comforts of context.

HE IS DAN, EAGER FOR FUN; HE WEARS A SMILE: EVERYBODY RUN

Like ethereal arch-villain "Bob" in David Lynch's *Twin Peaks,* Schreber (i.e., "Dan"), too, may function as an eternal recurrence (of pathology) spawned by (paternal) technology. In episode eight of the latest installment in the series, *Twin Peaks: The Return* (2017), the origin of Bob is seeded in the realization of the atomic bomb—Bob's existence/evil is a side effect of the development of this machinery of destruction, which is by default male, masculine, patriarchal, phallic. Dan is not evil, per se, but his identity hinges on the confrontation of numerous evil antagonists, and his origin (as a pathological superhero) can be traced back to the various machines into which his father plugged him, rendering him a certifiable rat in a Phildickian maze of death. Under the electric dome of the contemporary mediascape, we see Dan everywhere—his bellowing resounds up and down the hallways of popular culture, which has refined perception, desire and subjectivity to the degree that antiquarians from just 150 years ago might perceive us as extraterrestrial aliens in the right light. Consider the recurrence of the sun in musician Chris Cornell's lyrics.

Cornell mysteriously committed suicide in 2017, hanging himself in a hotel bathroom after a performance in Detroit, and his canon demonstrates a complex articulation of Georges Bataille's concept of the solar anus, an elliptical symbol for the mutable detritus that informs *Dasein* and that was anticipated in Schreber's *Memoirs*. In the following passages from songs written by Cornell for, respectively, Soundgarden, Audioslave and himself (as an independent artist), note the role of the sun:

"Black Hole Sun"

In my eyes, indisposed
In disguises no one knows
Hides the face, lies the snake
The sun in my disgrace
Boiling heat, summer stench
'Neath the black the sky looks dead
Call my name through the cream
And I'll hear you scream again
Black hole sun
Won't you come
And wash away the rain

"Shadow on the Sun"

And I can tell you why
People go insane
I can show you how
You could do the same
I can tell you why
The end will never come
I can tell you I'm
A shadow on the sun

"Nearly Forgot My Broken Heart"

Every time I stare into the sun
Trying to find a reason to go on
All I ever get is burned and blind
Until the sky bleeds the pouring rain

Every little key unlocks the door
Every little secret has a lie
Try to take a picture of the sun
And it won't help you to see the light

For Schreber, of course, the sun was much more than a volcanic shithole that drives you insane, denies you knowledge, or threatens to cleanse and/or castrate you. But his watermark is undeniable. Looking awry into the (sun)screens of liquid modernity will reveal a ubiquity of Dans, who, wearing smiles and seeking fun, have become immune to entropy as they suck the nutrients from God's excrement.

AVOWAL

My ability to not think that I am God is superheroic.

SCHIZROMANCER

Deleuze, Guattari and R.D. Laing "see psychosis as something childlike or Dionysian, though they then make the romantic move of valorizing rather than pathologizing these supposedly primitive and uncontrolled conditions" (Sass, *Paradoxes* 11). Note that romantic ideas about madness are typically not so romantic for the Wildman himself, who suffers in mind, body and "spirit."

ROOM 008-3

In the Insomnia Ward...

Sleep is evil, but to sleep is to live.

Sleep is a wild animal, a potent drug, a blood-starved vampire.

Ignore sleep, refute it, try to evade it, to kill it... and sleep will eat you.

If you do not take sleep, you will get the shakes and see things that aren't there.

Imagine a world without sleep. Image a body and biology and ontology that doesn't need or crave it.

There would be no more dreams, no more nightmares. No more unconscious interference.

SCHIZE: Terminal consciousness...

GÖTTERDÄMMERUNG

The German translation of *Ragnarök*, this term denotes a sequence of impending apocalyptic battles and natural disasters in Norse mythology whose aftermath is a proverbial New World. The English translation is "God's Dawn," or, "The Twilight of the Gods." Richard Wagner used the term for the final cycle in *Der Ring des Nibelungen*, beloved by Nietzsche as well as Hitler, the latter of whom doctored and injected the former's philosophy into the Nazi musculature like an anabolic steroid. As in the Old Norse tale, the cycle culminates in the downfall of gods and the primacy of two humans who will repopulate the earth, spawning a new and improved humanity that, following in the footsteps of Adam and Eve, is the product of incest (i.e., their children procreating with one another, their children's children following suit, etc.). Not surprisingly, Schreber channels *Götterdämmerung* into his diegesis and worldview. Citing Freud's case study, Eric L. Santner writes: "Recalling that Schreber had already alluded to the Wagnerian motif of a *Götterdämmerung* to characterize the end of the world, it is interesting to note that Freud reads Schreber's inner catastrophe as a variation of another Wagnerian scene of destruction and demise: 'An "end of the world" based upon other motives is to be found at the climax of the ecstasy of love (cf. Wagner's *Tristan and Isolde*); in this case it is not the ego but the single love-object which absorbs all the cathexes directed upon the external world'" (166).

DIE TOTENMASKE

From the Arcade: "The work is the death mask of its conception."
—Walter Benjamin, "One-Way Street"

AUF WIEDERSEHEN, IDÉE FIXE

I find myself increasingly upset by knee-jerk alienists, clinical futurologists and ontological engineers who operate under the impression that I am entirely delusional, psychotic and paranoid. As William S. Burroughs opines, "Paranoia is just having the right information" (qtd. in Morris 112). There is an energy that transcends reason and the body. I do not discount the possibility that I am not this energy. I am probably this energy, however, or at least its source material, making my manuscript a canny toolkit for existence in a multitude of worlds and time periods, even if God now exists in the form of auto-tuned rappers and reality television stars. These iterations are mere bundles of nerves, too, but God was more interesting when he was just an *idée fixe* in the sky.

THE TRANSCENDENTALIST MONSTER

As *Memoirs* progresses, Schreber's various readerships shift in concert with his m.o. and the flows of his desire. These readerships include family, friends, enemies, deities and humankind.

The success of *Memoirs* was not the product of a literary agent's tireless efforts and marketing strategies, but rather the notoriety of an innovative neurologist's essay and the scholarship and artistry incited by that essay.

Memoirs began as an extended *apologia pro vita sua* written for one reader: Flechsig/God. In the end, Flechsig/God had gone through several transformations until finally becoming Schreber/God, Lord of the Flechsigs, who also represented all of humanity, good and bad, male and female, living and dead, Christian and Schreberian. All binaries evaporated.

Several rogue scholars have argued that Schreber merely extrapolated and science fictionalized American transcendentalism, which has its origins in German Romanticism and revolved around the idea that the One could be found in (and effectively *was*) everything.

Consider this seminal assertion of identity in Ralph Waldo Emerson's essay "Nature": "Standing on the bare ground—my head bathed by the blithe air, and uplifted into infinite space—all mean egotism vanishes. I become a transparent eye-ball. I am nothing. I see all" (14).

Equally relevant is Walt Whitman, who, in "Song of Myself," asserts: "I am large, I contain multitudes" (88).

Schreber cranks up Whitman's dial (i.e., "I am the universe, I contain everything") while inverting the basic principle of Emerson's *Bildung* (i.e., "all mean egotism floods every shore and fills every depth"). Coupled with his gender trouble and rapier angst, he constructs a bona fide *id*-entity for himself and the realm of nature that he, a pathological technology of culture, has swallowed, digested and shit onto the firmament, pioneering eternity with his hotwired feces.

A core transcendentalist belief is that people are inherently good and pure. The problem is that they have been corrupted by social institutions and state apparatuses, but they can rebuild themselves, exhuming "goodness" from their territorialized bodies, by practicing self-reliance and making every effort to live independently from the Hoard.

SCHIZE: Schreber is a transcendentalist monster, a mechanized cultural *objet d'art* who remains as natural as a fat old man lying naked in the grass.

ROOM 007-3

I am not afraid to say my name in the dark.

Nor am I afraid of worms.

Or men.

Unmanned or not.

I am not who I am by virtue of who I am not.

Achtung. Outré.

Iamb.

MICROCRITICISM: SPECIAL AFFECTS IN *THE WOLFMAN*

Not to be confused with "History of an Infantile Neurosis" a.k.a. "The Wolfman," Freud's case study of Dr. Sergeï Pankejeff, a Russian aristocrat who suffered from depression and whose childhood dream of a tree full of wolves was psychoanalyzed as the traumatic effervescence of witnessing the primal scene, Joe Johnston's *The Wolfman* (2010), a remake of the 1941 film of the same name, bows to the terms of the Law of the Father, which afflicts the protagonist like a virus. In fact, Lawrence Talbot (Benicio del Toro) suffers from a terminal virus (lycanthropy) that he acquired from his estranged father, Sir John Talbot (Anthony Hopkins), who killed Lawrence's mother when he was a boy. Hence the father enacts the child's greatest oedipal fear: the murder of the opposite-sex parent, who he unconsciously desires. In order to achieve psychological resolution, the child must identify with the same-sex parent, i.e., he must become the father, which, in Talbot's case, entails becoming the wolf, too, but the wolf is superfluous and incidental to the triangulation of the son vis-à-vis the Freudian blot. The wolf is mere entertainment, a special *affect*. Or, if we must, it is just the (re)active but disposable primordial growl of the infantile subject.

PURE OCD

Also referred to as "primarily cognitive obsessive-compulsive disorder," this marginal variant of the dominant mental disorder is described by the OCD Center of Los Angeles as a condition in which the subject experiences "obsessions without observable compulsions. These obsessions often manifest as intrusive, unwanted thoughts, impulses or 'mental images' of committing an act they consider to be harmful, violent, immoral, sexually inappropriate, or sacrilegious. For individuals with Pure Obsessional OCD, these thoughts can be frightening and torturous precisely because they are so antithetical to their values and beliefs" ("Pure"). In the medieval era, OCD was naturally attributed to demonic possession (curable by exorcism or, in most cases, execution) and it wasn't until the turn of the twentieth century (punctuated by Freud) that it was more regularly attributed to neurological commotion, fissures, obstruction, latency, etc. The notion of pure OCD, on the other hand, originated with the explosion of media technologies in the 1960s and did not come into regular clinical usage until the twenty-first century. This isn't to say that primitive species didn't suffer from pure OCD (or more generalized OCD) in some form. Nobody notices a few errant sidewinders. It takes a legion to awaken a flock.

THIS IS MY WORLD

From the Reich: "The solipsist flutters and flutters in the fly-glass, strikes against the walls, flutters further. How can he be brought to rest? . . . But here solipsism teaches us a lesson: It is that thought which is *on the way* to destroy this error. For if the *world* is idea it isn't any person's idea. Solipsism stops short of saying this and says that it is my idea" (258, 255). —Ludwig Wittgenstein, "Notes for Lectures on 'Private Experience' and 'Sense Data'"

CONFESSION OF A CRAP ARTIST

I am only famous because I wrote a book about myself, possessed the wherewithal to have it published, and then somebody famous wrote about me after reading it. Remove your thick black spectacles and you will see that there are as many of Me in the world as there are stars in the universe.

ROOM 006-3

A mad hooker tries to scoop me off the shore with a shovel. Agog, I defragment her atoms and spread them across the crystal sea. I want to be here, all of my glands and digits flush against the cold concrete beach.

I monitor the jaundiced, bloated crabs that bob in the surf with my stalks. The smell of salt is potent.

Too fatigued to rearrange my corpuscles and put them in line. Too much vertigo. The mise-en-scène spins like a helix as it fades in and out.

"Where is the manuscript?" Squatting beside me, she traces the grooves of my cortex with a fingernail. "The manuscript is all that matters." Like a cephalopod, she emits an inky substance from the gills beneath her heavily veined breasts. It floats between us and encircles her. "You're feelings, your being, your worldview, your sense of self, your personal history, your inevitable future . . . turds. All turds."

I try to defragment her, but the ink protects her from my psychotropic aggression.

"There is no manuscript," I lie. "There never was."

UNVOLLENDET

This book was written backwards.

"*Rückwärts.*"

I began by writing it forwards.

"*Vorwärts.*"

I proceeded in this vein until the blood stopped flowing, then began at the end and ended at the beginning.

"*Anfang.*"

Retrospection is thus synonymous with schizophrenia. But I am not finished yet. The birds I feed continue to shout at me. Fewer and fewer lisp at me.

NOTES TOWARDS A NEUROMANTIC, NECROSPECTIVE CONSPIRACY THEORY

2100 A.D. (Define postapocalyptic setting.)

Condemning the influence General Freud exerted on western culture, namely his studies of pathology and psychosis, which were retroactively perceived as more detrimental than beneficial to the human condition re the primacy of sadness over happiness, the Directorate of Military Intelligence inserted Schreber (a.k.a. Insurance Agent Marx) into the German social matrix in the nineteenth century (sans tachyons), including his father, a spy and "father-thing" (ref. Philip K. Dick) whose task was to pathologize the "Son of Man," as he was referred to by British secret services. "To your scattered bodies go"—this rhetorical code sets Agent Marx to task whenever it is uttered by a Continental Op . . .

SCHIZOID MEME

Beyond "ego weakness," there is no universal theory that explains the root cause of schizophrenia. Before and after Schreber, origins remain a slave to subjectivity, like objective reality.

JARGONAPHASIA

Not mere preservation. And not without meaningful signification (insofar as any signifier has the capacity to make meaning).

Our insecurities, our defense mechanisms are always telling secrets in the dark even as they make spectacles of themselves in the light.

THE REAL

From the New Underworld: "The key words, the signifying words of Schreber's delusion, *soul murder, nerve-contact, voluptuousness, blessedness,* and a thousand other terms, revolve around a fundamental signifier, which is never mentioned and whose presence is in command, is determinant" (284).
—Jacques Lacan, *The Psychoses*

THE AFTERBURN

What initially piques readers about Schreber are the aberrations regarding his gender and sexuality. After close, careful analysis of *Memoirs* and secondary criticism, however, we forget about it. Or it becomes as mundane as the genitals with which each of us were born. The afterburn is purely cosmic. We molt our bodies and slither indefinitely across the bayou.

LIST OF ABORTED AND UNUSED CHAPTER TITLES

Hang 'Em Low. What Are You Thinking Now? Corpse Poison. Frank Vulgarities. *Dramatis Percolator.* Necessity Is the Mother of Invention. Signifyin(g) Birdies. The Poetry of Trauma. This, My Shit. Becoming-Woman/Womb. Picturing the Rays of Purity. Beyond Crucifixion. Having Intercourse with Myself. The Ideal-I. Like Sand through the Hourglass. To Empty Myself.

The Devil Can Crawl Through a Keyhole. Modus. Pathological Lucidity. Particularly on My Bosom. Flaming Speech.

SUPERZERO READERS

There is no readership for *The Psychotic Dr. Schreber*.

Correction.

There is a built-in readership of superzeros for *The Psychotic Dr. Schreber* whose interpellation in the Order of the World is a self-evident truth that only exists in subjective matrices.

There is only one true subjectivity.

Its name is Objectivity. Its doppelgänger is the big Other.

Ultimately the problem with reading is the reader, who is almost dead, but needs to die altogether. Only in the wake of the death of the reader can real innovation begin to spread its seed.

THE HISTORY OF THE WORLD

The history of the world is a cartography of the human mind, an unreliable narrator that effectively renders history a lie, which is a kernel of truth, i.e., truth in itself is a myth, a fiction that can only be approached through the vehicle of a large enough assemblage of like-minded lies.

NOW I LAY ME DOWN TO SLEEP

The elephant man died from the weight of his own head.

God died when Nietzsche "smote history into two halves" and kissed the future (Olsen 51).

But "God is not dead," says Baudrillard. "He has become hyper-real" (159).

What does this mean for the elephant man? Is he still standing naked on the hard rubber floor of the surgical theater? Is that a ghost, a hologram, a man or a monster? And why are all the doctors' backs turned? Why are they ignoring this freak of culture and futurity?

The rows of white coats explode into blackbirds that flutter into the rafters and choke on the dust.

There is no more sound. Finally.

Beyond the theater and the tundra, dark power plants loom over the ice canyons like broken reveries, billowing yellow smoke into the gunmetal sky.

THE PATHOLOGICAL MACHINE [PART 6]

In the end, *Dark City* functions as a critical analysis of *Memoirs* that illustrates how Schreber turns himself into God and subsequently turns everything and everybody into a malleable fiction as a means of compensation for the tyrannical psychotic forces that threaten to murder him spiritually, sexually, metaphorically and actually. Proyas' representation of the machinic city as God speaks to the pathological machine that Schreber becomes throughout his own bildungsroman narrative, which documents the maturation of his sublime identity.

ROOM 005-3

Anxiety strangles me . . . then releases me, once and for all, from its reptilian clutches. I never feel it again.

I never feel anything again.

I am the ghost of my former self.

No. I am more than a ghost of a simulacrum. I am the specter of history itself.

In effect, the future belongs to me.

HYSTERICAL OBITUARIES

7:02 p.m. Sipping a watered-down martini from a rocks glass, **Y** eases into a Naugahyde recliner, turns on the television and searches for *The Lawrence Welk Show*. He finds it; Welk is delivering his opening monologue.

The phone rings.

"Hello."

"What are you doing?"

"Watching *Lawrence Welk*. Who is this?"

"Did you read my obituary?"

"Are you dead?"

"I'll read it to you."

Y listens to the obituary. On the TV a woman with big blonde hair and deep cleavage sings a dance tune.

"That sounds fine, I guess. Who is this?"

Click.

7:22 p.m. The phone rings.

"Hello."

"What are you doing?"

"Watching *Lawrence Welk*. It's not very good tonight. Who is this?"

"Your corpse."

"Am I dead?"

"Did you read your obituary?"

"I don't read obituaries."

"Listen."

The obituary is read. On the TV a man with shoe-polish black hair in a periwinkle suit plays the piano and smiles a glassy white smile.

"A cause of death isn't cited. How did I die?"

Click.

7:59 p.m. The phone rings. Y is snoring.

10 p.m. The phone rings. Y stops breathing.

2:42 a.m. Y picks up the receiver and dials a number.

"Hello."

"It's me."

"What are doing?"

"Dreaming."

"What are you dreaming about?"

"*Lawrence Welk.*"

"What's happening in the dream?"

"People are smiling. People are singing. People are happy."

"How does it end?"

"With an obituary. It goes like this."

Click.

LEGION

"Indeed the Memoirs may be called the best text on psychiatry written for psychiatrists by a patient," write Hunter and MacAlpine. "Schreber's psychosis is minutely and expertly described, but its content is . . . fundamentally the same and has the same features as that of other mental patients. Schreber's name is legion...We have talked and listened to many Schrebers since we studied the Memoirs" (25). Moreover: "The content of Schreber's psychosis is not unique. Schizophrenics regularly are in doubt about the nature of their sex, commonly speculate on religious matters, particularly the end of the world, speak of sexual transformation, and live through pregnancy and birth fantasies. These last center around bowel function or the interior of the body" (407).

ROOM 004-3

In the dream, there is no autoscopy—everybody perceives and interprets the world through the polished lenses of their individual subjectivities, and all doppelgängers have been assimilated by the shadows of tomorrow.

The moon turns a blind eye to the stars. It is dawn.

The sun bends over and exposes her cloaca. It is dusk. This inspires another dream.

The cameraman uses 70mm film to record it. The dream is edited and then presented at a drive-in movie theater in Dreamfield, Indiana. The Director titles it *Wife*. Sitting in pickup trucks, smoking cigarettes and sipping canned beer, the audience watches it passively, remotely, evicted from themselves. Even the action scenes and special affects fail to vitalize them.

MOTHER [PART 1]

From the Machine: "Schreber is man and woman, parent and child, dead and alive: which is to say, he is situated wherever there is a singularity, in all the series and in all the branches marked by a singular point because he is himself this distance that transforms him into a woman, and at its terminal point is already the mother of a new humanity and can finally die" (77).
—Gilles Deleuze and Félix Guattari, *Anti-Oedipus*

MOTHER [PART 2]

Virtually nothing is known about Schreber's mother Pauline; all that has been written on and about her is, like psychoanalysis, speculative fiction. The only article of biographical material is a poem written by Schreber on the occasion of her ninetieth birthday. The poem is 435 lines long, including an addendum of seven vignettes that end with two riddles. The answers to the riddles are the names of houses that she lived in.

TERMINAL IDENTIFICATION

SCHIZE: Schizophrenia has evolved into a normative mode of consciousness. As such, Schreber speaks fluently the language of hermeneutics, technoculture, literary theory, the socius and many other disciplines, formations and (ir)realities. Additionally, any religion—and the reliance upon religion for sanity, for agency from the fear of death—makes as much sense as Schreber's peculiar riff on gnosticism/narcissism. As always, the loud flame needs the quiet ember.

FORGIVENESS

A Thin Man ambles down Prager Straße towards the train station breathing in the hybrid aroma of fresh bread, horseshit and pipe tobacco. Over 50 years later, in 1945, this very street will be fire-bombed by the Allies, who drop nearly 4,000 tons of high-powered explosives on Dresden, destroying the city center and immolating over 20,000 Germans. The Thin Man experiences this future memory, observing the flames dance across his skin and swim into his open throat. His organs catch fire and burn like prayers. Street performers, movie-goers and flâneurs point at the madman and gossip about his madness. He knows he can kill them. He can kill them more swiftly and effectively than the Nazi futurians that will succeed him, but he forgives them—he forgives all of them, the living and the dead, the unborn and the unbridled, the imagined and the erased—knowing he will assimilate the bodies, organs and souls of humanity into his nerves. Killing the other is as good as killing the self.

THE HIDDEN PERFECTION OF LANGUAGE

From the Café: "The marvelous logic of the mad which seems to mock that of the logicians because it resembles it so exactly, or rather because it is exactly the same, and because at the secret heart of madness, at the core of so many errors, so many absurdities, so many words and gestures without consequence, we discover, finally, the hidden perfection of a language" (95). —Michel Foucault, *Madness and Civilization*

HEIGHT

Moritz Schreber was five feet tall (Niederland 6).

FEET

Nothing can hurt my
feet if I put them through the
iron bars. They freeze.

ROOM 003-3

A polished skull rests on an accent table beneath a red lamp.

There is mucous on the carpet.

There is lightning in the corpus of the sky.

TORSO

These are not breasts. These are idle zones of intensity.

KOPFHALTER [HEAD HOLDER]

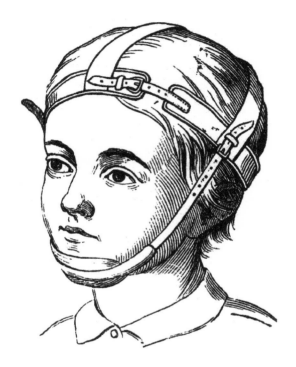

LAST WORDS

Scribbled vertically and horizontally on a notepad at a mental hospital in Leipzig-Dösen several months before his death, Schreber's last words required decipherment and included CAUSES, DAMNED, WRONG, DEBAUCHERIES and INNOCENT. The last word that he wrote down was POWER.

ROOM 002-3

This room, this organism, this apparatus, this monolith of rapture and cunt—it is an experiment. I have been vivisected by my Moravaginean dealer, who straddles me with a scalpel clenched between her teeth and tells me to fuck her as I conceptualize a dénouement. Distilled, I am a puddle of useless flaps. When I inhale, I become a dune of limitless power, colonizing the sky and terrorizing myself with my reterritorializations.

"Fuck me," she seethes through the blade. "Fuck me. Fuck me. Fuck me . . ."

ROOM 001-2

"Fort," I gurgle. "*Da* . . ."

POLLINATION

There is beauty in terror, beauty in theory, and beauty in the fiction of reality. Beauty in truth is harder to find in the factory or on the streets than in the tarn or on the fell.

Only beyond the rubric of time and sanity can we begin to pollinate these unburied flowers of evil.

END

THE SCHREBER CASE

NOTE: There are two editions of *Memoirs from My Nervous Illness* translated and edited by Richard A. Hunter and Ida MacAlpine. All citations of the main text in *The Psychotic Dr. Schreber* were taken from the 2000 edition published by The New York Review of Books.

"Addendum E: Judgment of the Superior Royal Court of Dresden of 14th July 1902." In *Memoirs of My Nervous Illness*, by Daniel Paul Schreber. 1903. New York: The New York Review of Books, 2000. 405-40.

Allison, David B., Prado de Oliveria, Mark S. Roberts and Allen S. Weiss, eds. *Psychosis and Sexual Identity: Toward a Post-Analytic View of the Schreber Case*. New York: SUNY Press, 1988.

Chabot, C. Barry. *Freud on Schreber: Psychoanalytic Theory and the Critical Act*. Amherst: The University of Massachusetts Press, 1982.

Dark City. Dir. Alex Proyas. Perf. Rufus Sewell, Kiefer Sutherland and Jennifer Connelly. New Line Cinema, 1998.

De Certeau, Michel. "The Institution of Rot." *Psychosis and Sexual Identity: Toward a Post-Analytic View of the Schreber Case*, edited by David B. Allison et al. New York: SUNY Press, 1988. 88-100.

Dinnage, Rosemary. "Introduction." In *Memoirs of My Nervous Illness*, by Daniel Paul Schreber. New York: The New York Review of Books, 2000. xi-xxiv.

Ferraro, David. "Biographical and Historical Background to Freud's Schreber Case." 2012. *Archives of a Divided Subject: Psychology and Psychoanalysis in the 21st Century.* 25 May 2013. Web. Accessed 3 Sep. 2017.

Freud, Sigmund. "Psychoanalytic Notes Upon an Autobiographical Account of a Case of Paranoia." 1911. *Three Case Histories.* New York: Collier Books, 1993. 83-160.

Hunter, Richard A. and Ida Macalpine. "Translator's Introduction." 1955. In *Memoirs of My Nervous Illness*, by Daniel Paul Schreber. Cambridge: Harvard University Press, 1988. 1-28.

Israëls, Hans. *Schreber: Father and Son.* Madison: International Universities Press, 1989.

Katan, Maurits. "Schreber's Delusion of the End of the World." *The Schreber Case: Psychoanalytic Profile of a Paranoid Personality*, by William G. Niederland. London: The Analytic Press, 1984. 121-25.

Lothane, Zvi. *In Defense of Schreber: Soul Murder and Psychiatry.* Abingdon: Routledge, 1992.

Lyotard, Jean-François. "Vertiginous Sexuality: Schreber's Commerce with God." *Psychosis and Sexual Identity: Toward a Post-Analytic View of the Schreber Case*, edited by David B. Allison et al. New York: SUNY Press, 1988. 143-54.

Mannoni, Octave. "Writing and Madness: *Schreber als Schreiber.*" *Psychosis and Sexual Identity: Toward a Post-Analytic View of the Schreber Case*, edited by David B. Allison et al. New York: SUNY Press, 1988. 43-60.

Niederland, William G. *The Schreber Case: Psychoanalytic Profile of a Paranoid Personality*. London: The Analytic Press, 1984.

Quinet, Antonio. "Schreber's Other." *Psychosis and Sexual Identity: Toward a Post-Analytic View of the Schreber Case*, edited by David B. Allison et al. New York: SUNY Press, 1988. 30-42.

Roberts, Mark S. "Wired: Schreber as Machine, Technophobe and Virtualist." *The Drama Review* 40.3 (Fall 1996): 31-46.

Santner, Eric L. *My Own Private Germany: Daniel Paul Schreber's Secret History of Modernity*. Princeton: Princeton University Press, 1996.

Sass, Louis A. *Madness and Modernism: Insanity in the Light of Modern Art, Literature, and Thought*. New York: Basic Books, 1992.

————. *The Paradoxes of Delusion: Wittgenstein, Schreber and the Critical Mind*. Ithaca: Cornell University Press, 1995.

Schatzman, Morton. *Soul Murder: Persecution in the Family*. New York: Random House, 1973.

Schreber, Daniel Paul. *Memoirs of My Nervous Illness*, edited by Richard A. Hunter and Ida MacAlpine. 1903. New York: The New York Review of Books, 2000.

————. *Memoirs of My Nervous Illness*, edited by Richard A. Hunter and Ida MacAlpine. 1903. Cambridge: Harvard University Press, 1988.

Weber, Guido. "Addendum B: Asylum and District Medical Officer's Report. In *Memoirs of My Nervous Illness*, by Daniel

Paul Schreber. 1903. New York: The New York Review of Books, 2000. 337-48.

Weber, Samuel M. "Introduction to the 1988 Edition." In *Memoirs of My Nervous Illness*, by Daniel Paul Schreber. Cambridge: Harvard University Press, 1988. vii-liv.

OTHER WORK USED

2001: A Space Odyssey. Dir. Stanley Kubrick. Perf. Keir Dullea, Gary Lockwood and William Sylvester. MGM, 1968.

Armand, Louis. "Alienist Manifesto." *Alienism* 1 (Oct. 2017): 1.

Artaud, Antonin. *To Have Done with the Judgment of God.* 1947. In *Selected Writings*, edited by Susan Sontag. Berkeley: University of California Press, 1976. 555-69.

Bacon, Francis. "Of Revenge." *The Essays.* 1597. New York: Penguin Books, 1985. 72-73.

Bataille, Georges. *Visions of Excess: Selected Writings (1927-39).* Minneapolis: University of Minnesota Press, 1985.

Baudrillard, Jean. *Simulacra and Simulation.* 1981. Ann Arbor: The University of Michigan Press, 1994.

Bauman, Zygmunt. *Liquid Modernity.* Hoboken: Wiley, 2000.

Bukatman, Scott. *Terminal Identity: The Virtual Subject in Postmodern Science Fiction.* Durham: Duke University Press, 1993.

Butler, Judith. *Gender Trouble: Feminism and the Subversion of Identity.* 1999. Abingdon: Routledge, 2006.

Canetti, Elias. *Crowds and Power.* 1960. New York: Farrar, Straus and Giroux, 1984.

Caputo, Philip. *A Rumor of War*. 1977. New York: Henry Holt & Company, 1996.

Cornell, Chris (Audioslave). "Shadow on the Sun." *Audioslave*. Epic, 2002.

——— (Solo). "Nearly Forgot My Broken Heart." *Higher Truth*. UME, 2015.

——— (Soundgarden). "Black Hole Sun." *Superunknown*. A&M, 1993.

Deleuze, Gilles and Félix Guattari. *A Thousand Plateaus: Capitalism and Schizophrenia*. 1980. Minneapolis: University of Minnesota Press, 2000.

———. *Anti-Oedipus: Capitalism and Schizophrenia*. 1972. Minneapolis: University of Minnesota Press, 1998.

Dick, Philip K. *A Scanner Darkly*. 1977. New York: Vintage Books, 1991.

———. "The Father-Thing." 1954. *The Philip K. Dick Reader*. New York: Citadel Press, 1987. 101-10.

Eliot, T.S. "The Love Song of J. Alfred Prufrock." 1915. *Collected Poems: 1909-1962*. New York: Harcourt, Brace & Company, 1991. 3-7.

Emerson, Ralph Waldo. "Nature." 1836. *Selections from Ralph Waldo Emerson*. Boston: Houghton Mifflin Company, 1960. 21-56.

Foucault, Michel. *Madness and Civilization: A History of Insanity in the Age of Reason.* 1961. New York: Vintage Books, 1988.

———. "This Is Not a Pipe." 1968. In *Aesthetics, Method, and Epistemology,* edited by James D. Faubion. New York: The New Press, 1998.

Freud, Sigmund. *Civilization and Its Discontents.* 1930. New York: W.W. Norton & Company, 1989.

———. "History of an Infantile Neurosis." 1918. *Three Case Histories.* New York: Collier Books, 1993. 161-280.

Hitler, Adolf. *Mein Kampf.* 1925. New York: Houghton Mifflin, 1971.

Kafka, Franz. "Letter to His Father." 1952. *The Sons.* New York: Schocken Books, 1989. 113-67.

Lacan, Jacques. "Science and Truth." 1966. *Écrits.* New York: W.W. Norton & Company, 2006. 726-45.

———. *The Ethics of Psychoanalysis: The Seminar of Jacques Lacan (Book VII).* 1959-60. New York: W.W. Norton & Company, 1997.

———. "The Instance of the Letter in the Unconscious, or, Reason Since Freud." 1957. *Écrits.* New York: W.W. Norton & Company, 2006. 412-41.

———. *The Psychoses: The Seminar of Jacques Lacan (Book III).* 1955-56. New York: W.W. Norton & Company, 1997.

Marx, Karl. *The Eighteenth Brumaire of Louis Bonaparte*. 1852. In *The Marx-Engels Reader*, edited by Robert C. Tucker. New York: W.W. Norton & Company, 1978. 594-617.

McLuhan, Marshall. *Understanding Media: The Extensions of Man*. 1964. In *Essential McLuhan*, edited by Eric McLuhan and Frank Zingrone. New York: Basic Books, 1995. 149-79.

Milton, John. *Paradise Lost*. 1667. New York: W.W. Norton & Company, 2004.

Morris, R.B. "I Am No Doctor." In *Naked Lunch @ 50: Anniversary Essays*, edited by Oliver Harris and Ian MacFadyen. Carbondale: Southern Illinois University Press, 2009. 107-13.

Nietzsche, Friedrich. *Ecce Homo: How One Becomes What One Is*. 1908. In *The Philosophy of Friedrich Nietzsche*, edited by Willard Huntington Wright. New York: Random House, 1954. 809-946.

Olsen, Lance. *Nietzsche's Kisses*. Tallahassee: Fiction Collective 2, 2006.

"Pure Obsessional OCD (Pure O)." *OCD Center of Los Angeles*. Web. Accessed 3 Oct. 2017.

Rickels, Laurence A. *Nazi Psychoanalysis: Volume 3 (Psy-Fi)*. Minneapolis: University of Minnesota Press, 2002.

Ricoeur, Paul. *Freud and Philosophy: An Essay on Interpretation*. 1965. New Haven: Yale University Press, 1977.

Rousseau, Jean-Jacques. *Confessions*. 1781. London: Penguin Books, 1953.

Sontag, Susan. Cover Endorsement. *Crowds and Power*, by Elias Canetti. 1960. New York: Farrar, Straus and Giroux, 1984.

Spider-Man. Dir. Sam Raimi. Perf. Tobey Maguire, Kirsten Dunst and Willem Defoe. Columbia, 2002.

The Birds. Dir. Alfred Hitchcock. Perf. Tippi Hedren, Rod Taylor and Jessica Tandy. Universal, 1963.

The Wolfman. Dir. Joe Johnston. Perf. Benicio Del Toro, Anthony Hopkins and Emily Blunt. Universal, 2010.

Tichi, Cecelia. *Shifting Gears: Technology, Literature, Culture in Modernist America*. Chapel Hill: University of North Carolina Press, 1987.

Twin Peaks. Dir. David Lynch et al. Perf. Kyle MacLachlan, Michael Ontkean and Mädchen Amick. Lynch/Front Productions, 1990-91.

Twin Peaks: The Return. Dir. David Lynch. Perf. Kyle MacLachlan, Michael Horse and Chrysta Bell. Showtime Networks, 2017.

Wells, H.G. *The Island of Doctor Moreau*. 1896. New York: Penguin, 2005.

Whitman, Walt. "Song of Myself." 1855. *Leaves of Grass*. New York: W.W. Norton & Company, 1973. 28-89.

Williams, William Carlos. "The Red Wheelbarrow." 1923. *The Collected Poems of William Carlos Williams*. New York: New Directions, 1986. 224.

Wittgenstein, Ludwig. "Notes for Lectures on 'Private Experience' and 'Sense Data.'" 1968. *Philosophical Occasions: 1912-1951.* Cambridge: Hackett Publishing Company, 1993.

D. HARLAN WILSON is an American novelist, short-story writer, literary critic, playwright, editor and university professor. He is the author of over twenty book-length works of fiction and nonfiction, and more than a thousand of his stories, essays and reviews have appeared in magazines, journals and anthologies across the world in multiple languages.

WWW.DHARLANWILSON.COM

OTHER BOOKS FROM STALKING HORSE PRESS

Jordan Rothacker *Gristle: Weird Tales*

duncan. b. barlow *A Dog Between Us,* and *The City, Awake*

Michael J. Wilson *If Any Gods Lived,* and *A Child of Storm*

Malcolm Mc Neill *Tetra: A Graphic Novel*

David Ohle *City Moon*

Emily Corwin *tenderling*

Quintan Ana Wikswo *A Long Curving Scar Where the Heart Should Be*

Jennifer Maritza McCauley *Scar On/Scar Off*

D. Foy *Patricide,* and *Absolutely Golden*

Jason De Boer *Annihilation Songs: Three Shakespeare Reintegrations*

Scot Sothern *BigCity*

Kurt Baumeister *Pax Americana*

Jessie Janeshek *The Shaky Phase*

Jennifer MacBain-Stephens *The Messenger is Already Dead*

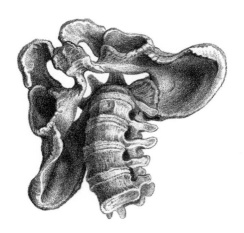

CPSIA information can be obtained
at www.ICGtesting.com
Printed in the USA
FFHW021555040619
52830609-58365FF